FIC   Luhrmann, Winifred
LUH   Bruce

Only brave
tomorrows

$13.95

DATE			

Only Brave Tomorrows

Only Brave Tomorrows

Winifred Bruce Luhrmann

Houghton Mifflin Company
Boston 1989

Library of Congress Cataloging-in-Publication Data

Luhrmann, Winifred Bruce.
  Only brave tomorrows / Winifred Bruce Luhrmann.
      p.   cm.
  Summary: In 1675 fifteen-year-old Faith comes from England to the
colony of Massachusetts, where the Indian uprising known as King
Philip's War threatens to destroy everything she holds dear.
  ISBN 0-395-47983-5
  1. King Philip's War, 1675–1676—Juvenile fiction.   [1. King
Philip's War, 1675–1676—Fiction.   2. Indians of North America
—Wars—1600–1750—Fiction.]   1. Title.
PZ7.L978160n   1989   88-13863
[Fic]—dc19   CIP
                               AC

Printed in the United States of America

P   10 9 8 7 6 5 4 3 2 1

For Skip

❧ Contents

❧ Historical Note

King Philip's War, 1675–1676

❧ King Philip's War was the most damaging war of American history. In 1675, King Philip, a Wampanoag Indian, united the various Indian tribes of New England to rebel against the colonists. The war lasted little more than a year, but it brought the colonies close to collapse. Twelve towns were completely destroyed and half of those remaining were severely damaged. More men died in proportion to the population than in any other American war. In Indian raids women and children also died, were carried off into captivity, or died of starvation or exposure to the elements.

Looking back at those times with the wisdom gained from distance, it is obvious to us that the war was inevitable. In the early days Indians were openly friendly as long as they were treated respectfully; but they gradually became aware that there was no way they could coexist in peace with the colonists. The number of colonists was growing, land was becoming scarcer, and differences in cultural expectations were extreme. It was becoming apparent to the Indians that only one people could survive in the land.

The Puritans had thought of themselves as the chosen people of God. By 1675, however, people were not as virtuous as they had been in the earliest days of the colonies. Was the war a sign from God that He was angry with them?

The many trials of these early colonists may have helped to fashion the strength of the New England character. Or perhaps the courage to venture to a new land brought to the colonies a type of people who were capable of rising above their troubles. To whatever we credit it, the characters of many of these early colonists make the stories of their lives fascinating to follow. Such a heroine was Faith Ralston.

Only Brave Tomorrows

1 ❧ A New World: October 1675

❧ "Land ahoy!"

The thin cry came from the lookout clinging to the mainmast far overhead. Faith craned her neck back until her long plait swayed against her skirts. The sailor's hand pointed west.

Faith hurried to the rail and peered across the gently heaving sea, squinting until she made out a faint dark line on the horizon.

Peter, the lad who had attached himself to her father during the voyage, wormed his way through the gathering crowd and came to stand next to Faith. Excitement overcame his shyness. "We're almost there!" he exclaimed, his large light eyes glowing, his mouth spread in a generous smile.

Papa appeared on the other side of Peter. "Not yet, my boy," he announced. "This land before us is known as the Cape. We have yet a way to go before we get to the port of Boston."

"How long?" asked Faith.

"Hours, just hours," proclaimed Papa loudly.

"Master Ralston, we have been so blessed to have come safely on this journey!" cried Peter fervently. "Won't . . ." He paused and swallowed with difficulty. It was not often that Peter spoke up. "Won't you please lead us in a prayer of thanksgiving?"

It had been a good journey, Faith realized gratefully. Though they had spent almost two of the eight weeks of their trip becalmed and many passengers had suffered constant seasickness from high seas, they had been fortunate. They had not suffered starvation or undue illness, been blown off course, or endured any of those ills that so commonly beset travelers.

A woman behind her spoke up: "Yes, sir, do." She pushed forward to talk with Papa and Faith slipped back toward the mast.

Papa's resonant voice declaimed, "O Great Redeemer, we kneel at your feet in thanksgiving and praise . . ."

Faith, uncomfortable, averted her face. She did not know whether to feel proud or ashamed that her father had taken it upon himself to lead the others. It was often the way she felt about Papa.

She looked back at him and sighed. His large, red-veined eyes were closed in prayer but his bald head was raised and the wind lifted the little wisps of greasy, gray hair above his ears. She was resentful that this man, this stranger who insisted she call him "Papa," and whom she had seen but once in her life before he had arrived at Auntie Abbie's house in Sussex just a few weeks ago, had insisted that she take this trip with him.

Her resentment even encompassed Auntie Abbie. Why hadn't she given him nay? All Faith's life had been spent with Auntie. Papa had gone to Holland right after Mama had died giving birth to Faith. "A religious exile," Auntie had called him. When he appeared in Sussex, Auntie had said to him, "It's about time you fulfilled your responsibility to the girl."

"That's what I have come to do," he had answered firmly. "I can provide a home for my child in the colony of Massachusetts and I want her there with me."

Never mind that Faith had been raised to be a proper lady. Never mind that she had been raised in a different religious conviction. Her father had arrived and demanded that she accompany him and the next day she had no choice but to travel with him to Plymouth to set sail for the New World.

She was so angry with Papa that she did not even want to believe in his God. Papa's God seemed like a different one than Auntie Abbie's. Auntie Abbie didn't talk a lot about God and make great claims for God's protection the way Papa did. But Auntie had, at bedtime the night before Faith had left, come to her and said, "Trust in the Lord, my child. No matter what happens, trust."

Gradually the crowd dispersed to prepare for the expected afternoon landing in Boston. The ship veered off from the end of the Cape and after a stretch of open

water came close to land south of Boston. As it continued up the coast through the early hours of the afternoon,
the view appalled Faith. The few tiny villages seemed
almost lost in the immensity of the forest. In most places
the woods came right down to the shoreline. The trees
were an endless green — mile upon mile.

At least it was an end to the journey — an end to
storms and alarms, the stench and discomfort, the constant irritations and lack of privacy.

"Boston!" announced Papa. He had come to stand
beside her, a short, bowlegged man, his arms folded
and the glow of a fanatic in his eyes. "Boston!" He
waved an arm expansively.

Boston? It was certainly a small town in comparison
to the bustling English port of Plymouth from which
they had sailed. And this was the colony's largest city?
Faith and Papa were headed for Springfield. How large
would it be?

By the time the boats had brought the passengers to
the dock, anticipation had worn her into exhaustion. The
passengers walked up from the dock, avidly stared at
by small children and an informal committee of Bostonians. "Welcome, welcome." Heads bobbed, curious
glances darted here and there, lips smiled. Faith's feet
slipped on the planking and a man's hand reached out
and steadied her. "Careful, girl."

Bostonians were friendly and curious for news of
England. They asked about the voyage, eager to find
out what manner of people had come to join them. Papa
was happy to talk with anyone. Faith had to tug him

along. "Please come, Papa. I do so long for a bath."

Before evening she had her wish. The landlady at the inn sent a maid with bucket after bucketful of warm water for a hip bath. Even Faith's hair could be washed and so cleanly that she stared at the strands as they blew dry in the sun and the breeze that came through the window of her room. She had forgotten how pale a brown her hair was.

Papa was almost drunk with the excitement of arrival. Faith could hear his voice all through the afternoon as he moved in and out of the ground-floor rooms of the inn.

Faith leaned out of her window, fascinated by the people in the street below. People here were so much more attractive than the people they had seen in Plymouth before leaving. She saw no beggars. Men stood straight and moved vigorously. Women were neatly and cleanly dressed.

She turned her head to the other side and blushed. A young man was staring at her, a wide smile on his handsome face. She was suddenly aware of her shift and the soft hair blowing across her face, and she withdrew immediately, embarrassed.

A knock came at her door. Faith hastily tied on a wrapper and opened it a crack. Peter stood there looking mournful. The corners of his mouth were turned down, his shoulders drooped, and his bulging, pale eyes were anxious.

"Your papa wants you to come to the inn parlor to meet your guide." He sighed. "My own relatives are not here. No one seems to have heard of them.'' His Adam's apple convulsed. ''Your papa wants you right away.''

''Peter, I'm so sorry.'' She didn't like Peter but she could imagine how he felt. ''You must stay with us until you find them. I'm sure Papa can help.''

''You don't mind?'' asked Peter, flushing.

She dredged up a smile and lied. ''Of course not.''

Her hair was still wet at the scalp but Faith ruthlessly dragged the comb through it and formed a tight plait. She dressed in a sadly wrinkled but clean flower-sprigged muslin which Papa had never seen and would probably disapprove of.

Papa, however, was so busy talking that he hardly looked at her. He was speaking with a rugged-looking man who Faith at first took to be an Indian. Not that she had seen any Indians close up, but Peter had pointed out a group in the distance when they had disembarked. None of them seemed to be as stocky and broad-shouldered as this man though, and the darkness of his skin surely came from the sun, for a paler skin showed around his neckcloth and sleeves.

. She stared at him haughtily. Even the commonest laborer at home knew enough to take off his cap in the presence of a lady. As if her thought had penetrated his mind, the man pulled off his fur cap and nodded to her, revealing that he had at least some semblance of manners.

Her attention was almost immediately diverted by the young man who stood behind him. It was the young man who had been looking up at her through the window. He now showed his appreciation of her appearance by the warm light in his bright blue eyes and the deferential bow he gave her as Papa, finally aware of her arrival, introduced him.

"This is Master Ralph Keene, Faith. Providence must have arranged for him to be with Sergeant Stedman at this time. Yes, Master Keene is the son of my friend, Samuel Keene, whose community we will be joining."

Papa went on delightedly. "I inquired for a guide and it was suggested by the landlord that I hire Sergeant Stedman here because he is setting out for his home in Springfield on Monday. Imagine my surprise when it turned out that Ralph Keene is also accompanying him!"

Faith curtsied to Ralph Keene but only nodded to the guide. Did one curtsy to someone who, at home, would have been a tradesman or a servant? She felt ill at ease. The appreciation of her appearance in the eyes of young Ralph Keene did not make up for the disapproval with which Sergeant Stedman was frowning upon her.

He spoke in a deep voice that startled Faith. "Young lady, I hope you are a sturdy walker. It is a long walk to Springfield and each of us will have to carry a share of the burden."

"A walking trip?" asked Faith, aghast. "We get to Springfield by walking?"

Sergeant Stedman seemed annoyed by her ignorance. "There is a trail to follow but only the sturdiest cart could handle it and a cart would travel so slowly that to try it would be dangerous."

Papa said, "Nor can we go by horseback. There are not many horses and I'm told those few need to be kept available for the militia."

"There is no point taking a horse if you are leading another animal," said Ralph Keene. Then, without further explanation, he went on, "We will not go all the way to Springfield, Miss Faith. We live in High Hills now. Springfield is a good ten miles further west. We lived in Springfield when we first came to the colonies but as soon as we got our allotment in High Hills we built our house there. Your allotment is waiting for you there."

"There is a community," said Papa hopefully. "There is a congregation."

"Not exactly. That is to say, there is a congregation but we do not have a minister to guide us. My father generally leads the service."

Papa seemed taken aback but he made a quick recovery. "I can be of assistance to him. I would be happy to do that."

Faith asked, "Is this a new community?"

"There are but four houses, all built in these last two years. If you build, that will be another and we expect more to join us before this year is out."

Papa nodded. Then he turned and put a friendly hand on Peter's shoulder to bring him forward. "This young man is Peter Eaton, who has come to be with his uncle in Springfield. Since his uncle has not come to meet him as expected, may he not join us on this trip?"

Ralph Keene's eyes went up and down Peter disparagingly. Sergeant Stedman asked, "Is your uncle named Clyde Eaton?"

Peter nodded eagerly.

Stedman shook his head. "I'm sorry, lad. Clyde Eaton died of fever last spring."

Peter's head jerked back. His eyelids fluttered and he swallowed convulsively. A chill ran through Faith as she realized how lost Peter must feel.

She rushed into words without thinking. "Papa, if Peter has no relatives to go to, can he not stay with us? Won't we need assistance in building our house? Can he not provide labor to make up for the lack of muscle that you so deplore in me?"

There was a long silence that seemed the louder for the bustle and activity going on around them in the inn. Papa drew a deep breath, but before he spoke Faith was already regretting her spontaneous offer. She was certainly sorry for Peter, but she had no desire to live with him.

Before she could shape a withdrawal, even before Papa spoke, Sergeant Stedman said matter-of-factly, "A strong back is welcome, Miss Faith, but the womanly skills are the ones more lacking in our communities: buttermaking, cheesemaking, baking, sewing, and all the domestic arts."

Papa scowled. "My daughter has been raised to be a useless ornament to society, I fear. Much of her time has been spent in pursuits which I cannot feel will benefit anyone. Her aunt saw to it that she had dancing and embroidery lessons and she was taught to paint pictures. The practical world is one she must learn."

Faith opened her mouth to protest. As if Auntie Abbie had not taught her plain sewing and how to keep household! She was willing to grant that perhaps she had some skills that were not going to be useful in this new world, but she would be surprised if anyone knew better how to cook a stew, roast a joint, or set up an herb garden.

The resentful words did not get spoken, for Papa was again talking. "Peter, it would give me great pleasure to have you join us. I have long wished for a son and you could help me as if you were one." He nodded and beamed.

Peter, stammering, tried to answer Papa. Sergeant Stedman cut in. "Excuse me, sir, but if we are to leave in two days I must go now and get busy. We will leave no later than Monday morning, no matter what the weather. With the Indians becoming increasingly hostile, there can be no delay."

He nodded his head curtly and hurried away, taking Ralph Keene with him. Faith stared after him. What a blunt, matter-of-fact sort of person the sergeant was. He had none of Ralph's charm.

"Hostile Indians?" quavered Peter.

Papa seemed not to have heard him.

Faith shuddered. "I expect we will hear more about them soon," she said.

2 ·§ *Setting Out*

·§ Faith, dressed for Sabbath meeting in her flowered muslin with lace ruffles, peered curiously into the windows as they walked along. On this early October morning Boston was a pleasant place: a fresh wind blew steadily from the harbor and sunlight heightened the red tones of the brick buildings. The salt sea air mingled with the riper smell of animals.

Faith and Papa were walking back from morning meeting accompanied by Peter and young Ralph Keene. Faith's stomach rumbled. She had missed breakfast and had been thinking about food all through the Reverend Increase Mather's sermon. She hoped that the inn provided a better noon meal than those she had eaten aboard the *Venture*.

Papa spoke, his voice carrying such stern disapproval that Faith was startled. "There are a great many Bostonians around who seem to be going about their daily business with no regard for the Sabbath." He shook his head solemnly. "Some I have spoken with are most disturbed by the increasing loss of religious devotion. When the colonists first came here everyone was expected to attend Sabbath worship, but the custom has not continued. I hear that the Reverend Increase Mather believes the loss of respect for God to be the cause of the troubles that have come."

"The troubles with the Indian called King Philip?" Peter asked.

Ralph nodded. "Reverend Increase Mather has said that unless we turn from our wickedness we will suffer, and he says the means God has chosen is this Indian uprising."

Faith had not been listening very attentively to the conversation up until now. "What Indian uprising?" she asked Ralph sharply.

"It's mostly King Philip and his Wampanoags along with the Narragansetts and the Nipmunks who have turned on us. They seek to drive the English out of these colonies."

In answer to her puzzled frown Ralph nodded firmly. "Yes, indeed. Many have died. It may be we will all have to live in garrisons if the Indians are not brought under control soon."

"Indians are killing just anybody?" The skin at the back of her neck prickled.

Ralph nodded again. He looked pleased to have a story that drew her full attention. "It all started in July. Since then the Indians have attacked the towns of Swansea, Rehoboth, Taunton, Mendon, and Brookfield."

"God is indeed trying his people." By the tremble in Peter's voice Faith could tell that he was as scared as she was.

She had been horrified to discover that they were going to be walking through the dangers of the forest to get to their new home near Springfield. The danger of enemy Indians made her fear of forest animals seem small by comparison. "Will it be safe to travel to High Hills?"

Papa, with unaccustomed kindliness, patted her arm. "The sergeant thinks we will be safe enough if we follow his instructions. And we are fortunate to have Sergeant Stedman for our guide. Our good innkeeper and even Ralph here say he is the best guide we could get."

"That is what my father says, Miss Faith." Ralph spoke to Faith but he looked at Papa. "Sergeant Stedman knows a lot about Indians. He even lived with Indians awhile when he first came to the colony."

Faith looked down. She wished she had as much confidence in the guide as the others did. From what she had seen of him she guessed he was no more civilized than the Indians were said to be, and no more trustworthy. For all they knew, he might feel friendlier to the Indians than he did to them.

After the noon meal Papa insisted that Faith go back with him for the afternoon service. The food had been good and the afternoon was warm. Faith settled back on the hard pew in hopes of a nap. A hard slap on the pulpit woke her up. The Reverend Increase Mather stopped slapping the pulpit and stared out over the congregation.

His hand was raised high and he seemed to be looking directly at her, his wide eyes dark in his pale face. He cried, ''You may think that this is a fight between the English and the Indians but I tell you — '' and here his voice dropped to a whisper, '' — I tell you, it is a war between God and Satan!''

He spoke so dramatically that Faith peered around the large room fearfully, wondering if the Indians would come in to attack and scalp them as they sat in their pews at worship. Could God really wish to punish his people in this way? She had so little piety that God must find her a shocking sinner.

What must it feel like to be scalped? Even on board ship, people had talked with hushed, horrified voices about that violent practice.

That night sleep did not come easily to Faith, and was fitful when it did. Faith was fortunate that in the women's sleeping room at the inn she had to share her bed with only one other woman. Her bed partner slept quietly but Faith stirred restlessly all night. Many times she rose and went to the window to peer fearfully into the dark street.

The next morning she did not awaken until Papa came into the room and shook her. He was annoyed. ''The rest of us have already broken our fast. Hurry, daughter. Do not shame me by your sloth.''

Buttons and ties seemed to elude her fingers. At last she got herself downstairs, but so late that the others were already getting their carrying baskets strapped onto their backs. The tanned, muscular guide looked like the

Indians in her bad dreams. She averted her face from him, shuddered at the suggestion that she eat, and prepared her bundles for the trip listlessly. Peter, Ralph, and her father were too engrossed in their preparations to pay much attention to her, but Sergeant Stedman looked at her searchingly. "Are you feeling ill, Miss Faith?"

She shook her head and lifted her load to show him that she was ready to start. To her irritation, it was already coming apart. The guide set to work on it. His broad, rough fingers were much more agile than her own when it came to knots and adjustments. He finally approved her preparations, checked over the others, and then asked them to wait by the front door of the inn. "Ralph, please bring around the cow."

"The cow?" Faith could not believe her ears.

"My father sent me to Boston to get a cow," Ralph said proudly before he hurried off. He reappeared around the corner with a rangy red and white cow who swayed as she walked. Faith tried to hide a smile as they set off through the streets of Boston to the stares of passersby. A company of little boys ran after them.

It was a relief to note that the animal could not set a very rapid pace. At least with the cow along, Faith, as the only female, would not be the one held responsible for slowing the group down. She shifted the weight on her back and wondered how, with such great burdens on their backs, and accompanied by a cow, they would escape if Indians set upon them.

Despite the easy pace, by noontime the boots Faith

wore had rubbed a blister across one heel. A brisk chill
was in the air, but the constant walking had made her
so hot that sweat ran down her back. Her waistband had
become so wet it rubbed to and fro, scraping her skin
until it was raw.

They stopped to rest at noon and Faith took off her
boot to examine her heel. Papa stared at the large blister
with distaste. It was Sergeant Stedman who came to her
assistance. After looking at the heel he said, "I always
carry an extra pair of moccasins." He sized her foot
against the soft leather and then proceeded to trim and
relace the moccasins to fit while she rubbed salve over
her heel.

"Did you make the salve?" she asked, sniffing its
unusual odor.

"That's bear grease and herbs you are smelling. An
Indian I know made it for me."

"An Indian!" she exclaimed and glared at the salve
as if it might bite her.

"Indians make the best salve," he said curtly. He
paused slightly and went on. "I have a friend named
Wannalancet. He once saved my life when I injured
myself in a fall from a cliff. He has since indirectly
saved my life many times by all I have learned from
him."

"Oh," she said. What manner of man was this?

Now that she was able to walk without limping she
could observe her companions. As they went along she
could see that Papa was trying to match the easy stride
of the guide, but it looked to her as if Papa might have

a blister also. He was certainly walking with an odd wobble. He was so short it was difficult for him to keep pace. The guide seemed taller than the others but was actually no taller than average. She decided that he appeared to be large because his shoulders were so broad. Ralph and Peter looked like long beanpoles beside him. She envied the long legs that made it possible for them to move along quickly.

She sighed deeply. Sergeant Stedman turned around to gaze curiously at her. She wondered what he thought of them all.

By midafternoon Faith had to struggle to hold herself erect. It was a constant effort to focus on the view ahead. Surely, she felt, there were more hours in this day than in any other she had ever lived. Later in the afternoon her feet felt as if they were on fire, her knees ached so painfully that she bit down a moan with every step she took, and she thought she had never been in such utter misery; Sergeant Stedman turned around to study the condition of them all and said, "Miss Faith is keeping pace better than either of you lads. Can you not even keep up with a young maid and a cow?"

Papa, whose exhausted, staggering progress had been tactfully overlooked, said proudly, "It is good stock my daughter comes from, it is. Her mother was a fine lady and as brave as they come."

Between these two comments, both so unexpected, Faith found the strength to move on and to hold back the bitter comments that had been festering inside her. Peter, his pale, drooping features drooping even more with fatigue, attempted to grin at her but only managed a sorry grimace. Ralph, who was lagging behind them all, scowled and turned his face toward the deep woods.

Gradually hunger was added to the physical pains that beset Faith. She noticed with relief that the sun was lower on the horizon and the woods were throwing deeper shadows. The cow came to a stop and mooed. Sergeant Stedman slapped her flanks until she moved on again. He looked up and caught Faith glaring at him. "Best break for the night soon," he said. "We aren't much further than Dedham, but the cow won't be able to go much more tonight. There is a spring up on the next hill. We'll camp there for the night."

"If we aren't far from Dedham, why don't we over-night there?"

He shook his head. "We will bring too much attention to ourselves if we stop off in a community. Wherever there are a few houses and some trading, you find an Indian or two hanging around—let any of them see us and the information about our trip will get around to undesirables in no time. Fortunately there were no Indians around as we left Boston. The trail we are taking is not often used. We are traveling so slowly that I want to avoid towns if at all possible."

His words sent a shiver down Faith's back. She threw a grateful look at the cow. He thought this was traveling slowly? "How long would it take to travel without the cow?"

"By myself, depending on conditions, I walk twenty-five to sixty miles a day. We won't be doing more than two or three miles an hour.''

She noticed that the sergeant was watching Papa as carefully as she was. Papa's head gleamed with sweat in the waning light, his eyes looked more yellow than ever, and he had ceased talking hours ago.

The gentle hill toward which they were headed began to look like an impossible mountain. She shifted the load on her back once again and set one foot in front of the other. After what Papa had said she was definitely not going to complain.

3 ❧ *Under the Stars*

❧ Though the setting sun spread a wide band of orange-red across the sky, fatigue wiped the color from the evening. Faith saw only the capped head and sturdy shoulder of the guide silhouetted against the sky as he moved forward ahead of them. Then, even that view was blurred as the sweat dripped into her eyes. She lifted a weary arm and wiped it across her face. Sergeant Stedman turned and smiled encouragingly.

It was the first time she had seen him smile at all. His whole face changed, the stiff lines of his nose and jaw softening. She swallowed hard and smiled back uncertainly.

"That's it," he said, pointing, "the goal of today's trip. That stand of pines. You see the three of them in a row? I often camp here. It has a spring, good sleeping on pine needles, and also a good lookout."

"Did your friend Wannalancet show this to you?" asked Faith.

He shook his head. "He never showed this to me, but he taught me what to look for when camping."

With a few more steps they were there. She watched gratefully as the sergeant turned to take the bundle from Papa's back. Relieved of the burden, the older man tried to smile but failed miserably. "Lie down here, sir," ordered the guide, kicking a pile of dry pine needles together. "Your inactivity aboard ship has ill prepared you for a trip such as this."

Papa's head slid slowly over the pile of needles until he was comfortable. He closed his eyes and seemed to sleep. Faith sighed and flexed her arms and shoulders. She had never before realized there were so many parts of the body to hurt.

The cow started wandering back down the hill. Faith went after her and took her to the stream running down from a spring that gurgled out from a cave of granite. The cow shoved her nose in eagerly. Faith almost did the same thing. She filled her hands and drank deeply, then splashed the cold water over her hot cheeks.

Peter took off his boots and hose preparing to chill his feet when their guide snapped angrily, "Not here! We drink here. Wash your feet down below."

Ralph and Peter soaked their feet. Faith tied the cow and came to eat. "Aren't we going to have a fire?" she asked with surprise as Stedman cut the brown bread into squares and broke off hunks of the hominy. He carefully set bread and hominy and a small dried fish on each of five comfrey leaves.

"We have plenty of food. We don't need to risk a

fire.'' As she stood uncertain, tempted to join Peter and Ralph at the edge of the stream, he added, ''Don't forget that the night will quickly cool us off. It is into October. Chilled feet are uncomfortable on a cold night.''

They all gathered around the food. Even Papa roused himself to eat.

''No ale?'' asked Peter.

''We had enough to carry without it,'' said Sergeant Stedman. ''The water is good.''

''I never drank water until coming here,'' said Peter. ''The water we have at home is brackish.''

Enthusiasm roused Papa to more life. ''In this country the water is pure as the land is pure,'' he said happily. He thumped his chest. ''It is a pure water in a land where the hearts and souls of the people are as pure and fresh as its crystal water.''

Unfortunately he noticed the rolling eyes that so rudely expressed Ralph's response to his florid statement. He stared in shocked astonishment that was made worse by Faith's helpless giggle. Sergeant Stedman frowned and said, ''We will do very well with water. 'Tis best for those who travel a lot not to become too dependent on any one food or drink for it may not be always at hand.'' He looked sternly at Faith. ''Eat, Miss Faith, or you will not be able to manage the journey tomorrow.''

Hungry though she was, Faith found the dry bread difficult to chew. Peter watched as she worked away at it. ''The fish is good,'' he suggested helpfully, and she found it was. The hominy was tasty also.

''We have not thanked the heavenly father for this

meal,'' said Papa as he carefully swallowed his last bite.

Sergeant Stedman sat back on his feet and crossed his arms over his chest. ''You had best do that for us, sir,'' he said.

Faith took care not to look at Ralph as Papa prepared to address the deity. Praying was one of Papa's favorite activities. He liked praying loudly, and he did so now.

''Shush,'' warned Sergeant Stedman.

Papa ignored him.

''Shush,'' said Sergeant Stedman more firmly.

Papa stopped, opened his eyes, and stared, astounded, at the guide.

''We are trying to pass through the forest without bringing attention to ourselves,'' Stedman pointed out in a gentler, more respectful tone. ''You have a fine, resounding voice, Master Ralston. It could be a danger to us.''

After a moment Papa resumed his praying, making up for his lack of volume in florid praise of the ability of their guide, the beauty of the landscape, and the opportunities in the new land. A choking sound from Ralph enticed Faith to peek at him out of the corner of her eye. He was giving her a sideways look, hoping to attract her attention by aping the crossed arms and up-right carriage of the guide. His handsome face was fixed in mock seriousness. Faith's shoulders shook with laughter.

Papa went on and on. Faith did not know what was wrong with her. Now that she had started laughing she could not stop. Ralph looked pleased to be so amusing.

Faith turned her head aside and screwed her eyes shut. She really did not like Ralph so well anymore. She twisted her head further away and took a quick look at Sergeant Stedman. He was watching her laugh at him. Abruptly the giggling fit stopped. It seemed forever before Papa finished talking to God.

It was now quite dark. Without a word the guide rose and, with a stick, scraped a pile of dry fragrant needles into a large bed beside the rock wall of the hill. He tethered the cow to the tree that rose in the middle of the bed and showed each of them how to roll a blanket so that it stayed warmly around them yet would allow them to leap up suddenly should they need to.

"Sleep as close together as possible," he said. Ralph and Peter were to sleep on one side of the cow. Faith, Papa, and Sergeant Stedman were to sleep on the other.

"Won't the cow attract wildcats?" asked Ralph. "Shouldn't we have a fire?"

"No. Cows usually settle down well after dark. If she makes a fuss and wildcats come, then we will build a fire. I do not wish to risk attracting attention from Indians unless we have a serious problem."

The cow lay under the pine in the moonlight, chewing her cud. Faith rolled herself near enough to the cow to feel some of its warmth. October nights were indeed cold. She shivered in her blanket until Papa settled next to her. He smelled ill. She noticed that Sergeant Stedman on the other side of Papa had his head turned away from Papa's odor. She also noticed that he had his rifle tucked under his shoulder where he could grab it instantly.

The moonlit sky was bright, but the canopy of pine branches cut out most of the light. The wind soughed overhead. Small night animals made scampering and squeaking noises. Certainly those weren't wildcats. Ralph said that wildcats screamed. Before long she could hear Papa's loud snore. Sergeant Stedman rose on his elbow and gently rearranged Papa. The snoring subsided. Soon there was even breathing from Peter and Ralph as well as Papa. Why couldn't she hear Sergeant Stedman sleeping? Cautiously she lifted her head and peered at him.

"Go to sleep, Miss Faith," he said in a low tone.

Despite her fatigue, Faith's mind kept dwelling on all she had seen and done. She wondered if Auntie could possibly imagine the type of life she was facing. Already Faith felt as if she had become a different person from the girl who had arrived in Boston.

During the day Ralph had told of Indian atrocities that could happen to them, and the sergeant confirmed that much of Springfield, where his home was, had just been attacked and burned. Ralph only ceased talking of Indians to mention horrors such as getting lost in the wilderness, freezing in the winter, suffering starvation, or being attacked by bears and catamounts. Nothing in Sussex had prepared her for this.

Papa had taken to repeating "Trust in the Lord" every time Ralph presented a new horror. Auntie used to say the same thing sometimes. Papa and Auntie had different approaches to God, but both had strong beliefs.

Faith had never really thought too much about religion before. Did she need a strong faith for the courage she must have to deal with life here? She gazed up into the stars and wondered.

On a far hill a fox barked. She shivered all the more. Suddenly the moon on its course broke through a gap in the branches above her. She stared into its cold yellow light. Gradually her fears began to leave her. This was the first night in her life that she had slept without a roof over her head. Despite the fearsomeness of it, it was incredibly beautiful. For a while she listened to the wind. Then she slept.

4 ❧ High Hills

❧ The morning sun, angled through the branches overhead, broke Faith's sleep. The air was cool and crisp and she hated to move from the warm nest in which she was curled. Turning her head she saw that Sergeant Stedman had already left his bed. A sound from downstream showed him guiding the cow for her morning feeding. Faith moved quickly and quietly. She wanted to be up and washed before the others awoke.

The water from the spring was so cold it made her gasp. She cupped her hands and drank from them, loving the mineral tang of the water. Then she combed her hair, a task that required patience. Tiny twigs and pine needles had dropped into it during the night.

When all but Papa had awakened, she roused him, shaking his shoulder and calling to him. All of them looked tired from the day before, but Papa was drawn and gray, his round eyes an unpleasant yellow. He was unusually quiet as they ate, devoting all his energies to eating.

Sergeant Stedman took Ralph and Peter aside and pulled open their bundles, talking to them all the while in an undertone. Then he unwrapped Papa's bundle and split his supplies into two piles. These he joined with the supplies each young man already had. He showed them how to tighten and lash each bundle into the back baskets. Now their backpacks were almost as large as his.

"I would like to carry some of Papa's supplies," protested Faith, disturbed that she had not been given any of the load.

"You cannot carry too much at the present, Miss Faith, for I want you to be free to carry the provisions if I have to leave you suddenly."

At her shocked expression he went on, "If a militia-man comes upon us on the trail I may have to leave with him. A scouting party of the militia may be in greater need of my help than you folks. I will, of course, give Ralph full instructions for the rest of the trip. He should know the route well, having taken it many times. Since I must be free to leave, I can carry none of your father's supplies and you, Mistress Faith, must be able to take over carrying the provisions."

"You might leave us?" asked Papa anxiously. He had watched the preparations with lackluster eyes and yet had not, to Faith's surprise, made a comment on them.

"Ralph Keene has been over this trail many times," said the sergeant again. "He should be able to take over if I leave."

"But we hired you," protested Faith, aware of the gulf of experience and ability that lay between Ralph and the guide.

The features of the guide looked even more wooden than usual. "The welfare of the militia is of the greatest importance to all of us. If they need me, I must go."

Faith bit her lip. She wished she could tell him that she would not be so worried if it were not for Papa's weakened condition. What help would Ralph be if Papa got weaker? She tried to strap on her basket but her fingers seemed to be all thumbs. Sergeant Stedman came over and, his fingers moving skillfully, quickly fastened the straps.

In a low voice he said, "If I must leave, you are to see to it that young Keene does not hurry your party along too rapidly. Your father will manage if the pace is slow and regular. Don't strain him."

Faith nodded. He looked down at her. "You should be proud of yourself, Miss Faith. You are a good traveler." The unexpected praise was so surprising that she felt herself blushing with pleasure. She nodded again and smiled back, feeling oddly shy. The guide was a strange man, she thought, abrupt and almost rude at times but kind and thoughtful when it most mattered.

The sun had risen considerably since they had awakened and with it came greater warmth. As they moved along the trail the protest of her muscles was all she noticed at first, but as time went on the sun dissipated the chill of the night and much of the ache in her limbs.

Today, despite painful aching, she was ready to swing along faster, longing to reach the end of the journey and of discomfort.

Ralph and Peter were also eager to move along rapidly and were out of sight before the others had climbed the first rise. It was the guide who held them back. "Walk at an easy pace, sir," he said to Papa. "Your lack of experience is beginning to catch up with you. Don't let the young folks move you along faster than you wish to go."

Papa gave a brief, artificial smile. "Well, I can understand their urge to move as rapidly as possible. I also wish . . ."

"You would be foolish to go faster than you are now going," said Sergeant Stedman, the tone of his voice harsh and uncompromising. "We have almost seventy miles yet to travel. If you are worn out, who will carry you? Don't forget, if the cow arrives worn, she cannot give milk. Common sense must rule the day, Master Ralston."

Faith voiced the fear she had been living with. "How much food do we have? How long will it last?"

"Five days. If we see that the trip will take more time we must apportion out the food accordingly. There is little time for me to hunt, and if I should leave you, you must not waste any time at all doing so."

As the day wore on, the aches and pains from the first day of travel seemed to multiply. The strained, white look on Peter's face and the gray cast of Papa's complexion told Faith she was not the only one suffering. "The muscles do not protest so much when they become accustomed to the trail — is that not so?" Papa asked Sergeant Stedman, his voice not quite steady.

"Some people become accustomed to trail walking in a very short time. Those who have been shut up aboard ship for some time take longer." He evidently felt more encouragement might be needed. "Those who live here do enough physical work to keep from aching with activity such as this."

Faith's eyes widened. In other words, there would be little rest to look forward to at the end. The picture of herself as she had been the day Papa arrived in Sussex — charmingly attired, daintily embroidering under the chestnut in Auntie Abbie's front yard — flashed into her mind. Papa was right: she was poorly trained for the life they would have here. She looked down at her arm. The wrist was dirty, the sleeve of her dress too short, and the arm itself thin. She had always been thin, but shipboard life had dulled her appetite so that she had lost even more weight. She did not like thinking of how meager her looks might be. And how her feet did hurt!

She wondered what Auntie Abbie would say if she could see her niece now. Faith smiled grimly. Auntie Abbie would probably say she was glad she had not raised a complainer. Faith gritted her teeth and kept on.

They toiled up over the crest of a hill and came upon a meadow, startling a herd of deer who bounded away leaving a faint fragrance of crushed thyme behind. The deer had been gathered around a salt lick. Sergeant Stedman guided Bossie over to it and told them to rest while they waited.

Faith walked over to the edge of a brook and perched herself on a rock. Signs of the coming cold could be seen in the scarlet of the sumac and the yellow-veined leaves of the birch. England had never been so colorful. While she sat, a cloud obscured the sun for a few minutes. Faith looked around uneasily, for the first time visualizing how it would be on their trip if rain came.

It did not rain that night or the next. Progress along the trail continued steady, if slow. It was not until early Thursday that there was a change in the weather. A brisk wind heralded the change, snapping the leaves off the trees so that the air was full of them. The temperature dropped and a spatter of raindrops came on gusts of wind. Within minutes a drizzle began and continued the rest of the day.

With her head down against the rain Faith did not at first see the men on the trail ahead of them. When she did look up she would not have identified them as militiamen if it had not been for Ralph's whispered commentary. The three of them were dressed in unidentifiable garments that had become so coated with mud they seemed glued to the men. They were unshaven and their weatherbeaten complexions made them look as dark as the Indians she had seen in Boston. She saw them glance curiously at her and there was little in her appearance that they missed, from the sodden plait that hung limply down her back to the hose that drooped over the soaking moccasins on her feet.

The event she feared had arrived. The men had come from Boston and were on their way north, beyond Springfield, to Deerfield where there had been a major Indian attack. They did not want to keep to the trails and they needed to travel rapidly. They needed the sergeant to guide them.

She stood patiently, feeling like a beast of burden, while the guide repacked her basket, filling it with the provisions he had been carrying.

Sergeant Stedman spoke briefly before leaving them. "Keep to the southern trail. I don't want you on the more northerly trail because it is best to stay well away from Brookfield. There has been too much trouble there."

"Surely by now . . ." began Ralph.

"It is unsafe." The guide's face was grim. "You are unlikely to be able to light any fires in this rain, but don't even try to. In ordinary times Indians seldom use this trail. Right now I'd make no assumptions at all. Don't do anything to bring attention to yourselves."

"How do we sleep in the rain?" asked Faith, for a chill had settled in her back and feet and she wanted nothing as much as a warm, dry bed.

"About three miles along on this trail there is a cave that is almost always dry. Bed there for the night."

Ralph protested again. "So soon? We could get a lot farther before dark."

"There is not another good cave between here and High Hills. There aren't many miles left to your trip, but too many to make it to the finish tonight. Bed in the cave and you will arrive in High Hills tomorrow."

Ralph scowled but said no more. Faith, watching Papa, was relieved that there would soon be an end to today's trip. Papa was looking more wizened than ever, his back more bent and his steps more hesitant.

When she looked back, the militiamen and the sergeant were gone. A sense of desolation hit her. With the sergeant in charge she had little fear of Indians, wild animals, or any other danger. Without him . . . A quiver of fear ran across her shoulders. The words of Auntie Abbie came back to her: "Trust in the Lord." Just saying them over brought a measure of calm. After all, God had brought them safely across the ocean and things had gone well thus far.

She looked around. Her three traveling companions were already walking ahead, Peter plunging on and looking as miserable as he had at the start of the trip, Papa moving with slow, dogged determination, and Ralph sulkily tugging Bossie along.

She caught up with Ralph intending to ask him a number of questions. She was not surprised that he started complaining at once. "If he left me in charge he should have allowed me to make the decision about where to camp and how fast to travel. He isn't going to be here so he doesn't care if we dawdle. Did you see how fast they moved when they went off?"

Sometimes Ralph was so self-centered that he reminded her unpleasantly of the worst in herself. "Probably all those men are healthy," she said tartly, but softly enough so that Papa would not overhear her. "We didn't pay for a guide for the guide's convenience, Ralph

Keene, but for my papa's. He can't possibly go much farther today. Did you have it in mind to carry him on your back along with your basket?''

He shot her a look of dislike. ''And keep your rifle dry,'' she added with exasperation. ''What if you need to use it?''

He paused and with a glare at her, swung it around so that water would be less likely to penetrate the barrel. ''Yes,'' she said, ''that's the way Sergeant Stedman carries his.''

''It's at the wrong angle for comfort,'' Ralph pointed out, aggrieved. ''It hits me with every step when it hangs like this.''

Faith raised her eyebrows but said no more. The longer she knew Ralph the less appealing he became.

Before long they reached the cave and, as Sergeant Stedman had said, it was dry and surprisingly warm. Even without a fire she found herself beginning to dry off. She examined the dry leaves and needles that were piled to one side and smoothed them down for Papa. ''Lie down and rest, Papa,'' she said. ''I will be setting out food in a few minutes, but lie down and rest until I have it ready.''

He stiffly lowered himself. Within moments he was sleeping. She had not the heart to awaken him for his food.

''He is still dressed in all his wet things,'' said Peter. ''Shouldn't we get him dry and wrap him in his blanket instead of that wet cloak?''

He unpacked the blanket and handed it to Faith, but

the blanket was so wet it dripped. Faith's own blanket was still mostly dry. She and Peter carefully removed the sodden cloak and wrapped the old man in the dry blanket. ''The clothing next to his body may be starting to dry already,'' said Peter hopefully. He wiped the end of his dripping nose with his elbow and sighed. ''And what will you do for the night without a blanket?''

''I will roll up to his back as close as possible,'' she said doubtfully. She spread the wet cloaks as widely as space would permit. It was not really warm enough to dry them by morning but perhaps some of the weight of water would be gone.

Ralph came back inside after tending to Bossie. In the enclosed space there was a strong odor of drying wool and cow.

Morning brought no improvement. The drizzle of the day before had turned into a steady downpour. Vision was so difficult that Ralph kept losing the trail and their progress was painfully slow.

''The sergeant said you knew this trail,'' said Faith, exasperated.

''Of course I know this trail,'' exploded Ralph. ''We are only a mile or two from home but the blazes that mark the trees are difficult to see in the rain.''

Faith longed for the reliable leadership of the sergeant. At one point poor Bossie stubbornly stood to moo her melancholy. It took both Ralph and Peter to tug her back into motion. Every time Ralph lost the trail he became more irritable.

It was getting dark when Ralph gave a grunt of relief.

"Praise the Lord," he announced grimly. Faith looked ahead and saw they were at last entering a clearing. She looked across at the first dwelling she had seen in five days. When Papa and Peter also said "Praise the Lord," she joined them.

The welcome was all they could ask for. All the little community filled the Keenes' small house to greet them. Faith was aware only of the members of the Keene family: Master Keene, an older version of Ralph with his handsome features and bright blue eyes and charm; Mistress Keene, a worn woman who looked more like Master Keene's mother than his wife; and twin boys who were appallingly exuberant. She was too tired and confused to sort out the neighbors who came in. She was interested only in the warm fire and dry clothing.

Papa, too exhausted to talk with his old friend, was immediately put to bed in the bedstead in one corner. Peter went up the ladder to sleep with the Keene boys, his face looking haggard.

Faith lay down in her blanket before the fire next to the Keenes' large black dog, Moses. Her last thought was, "Auntie Abbie, if you could only see me now. . . ."

5 ❧ New Beginnings

❧ Faith woke abruptly. The sharp shake of her shoulder had frightened her. For a moment she thought she was still on the trail with danger all around. It took a moment of blinking to recognize the worn face peering down at her, the eager smile showing a number of blackened teeth and empty holes.

"Mistress Keene!" She struggled to sit up. Mistress Keene still had a hand on her shoulder. Faith could hear Master Keene snoring over in the bed in the corner opposite Papa. Overhead in the attic there was silence. Gray morning light crept through the chinks of the cabin and the cold hearth smelled stale.

"It's time for the women to get up!" exclaimed Mistress Keene brightly.

Faith frowned and blinked again. Chill air crept down her back. "Are the boys up and gone?" she asked, wondering why it was so quiet.

"Oh, no!" exclaimed Mistress Keene, shocked at the idea. "They be all wore out what with their getting cold and all. No, indeed, they be sleeping yet."

"They are?" Faith was indignant. "Mistress Keene, they aren't the only ones tired. My papa was all wore out and I — "

Mistress Keene interrupted happily. "It is so good to have another female around. There's days I'm that tired I can't hardly climb out of bed in the morn. It's a real joy to know there's someone to help feed and care for all the family."

These words so appalled Faith that the last cobwebs of sleep dropped abruptly away. She rose from her pallet and adjusted her clothing without any awareness of the cold and discomfort of the morning. "Mistress Keene," she began to say firmly when the older woman shushed her.

"We don't want to wake them up now, do we?" she adjured Faith sternly.

"Don't they have work to do, too?" asked Faith in an only slightly more subdued tone. "Don't they have to feed the animals and start the fire?"

"You can start the fire." Mistress Keene frowned at her. "The animals can wait until after we break our fast."

"I don't know how to start a fire," said Faith untruthfully.

The lines on the older woman's face drooped. Her expression became bleak. "I'll have to teach you." She sighed.

Faith set her chin stubbornly. "Ralph knows how to make a fire."

Mistress Keene's grayed brows met in stern disapproval. "He was looking that weary last night! I like to spare him when I can."

She knelt painfully on the edge of the hearth. As she reached toward the coals Faith remembered that she had noticed last evening that the woman seemed to have difficulty in moving her joints. Seen in profile it looked as if she had once been a pretty woman. Pain, illness, and perhaps sheer hard work now made her look older than Auntie Abbie.

"Why?" asked Faith.

The woman turned to Faith, puzzled.

"Why does Ralph have to be spared from morning labor? He seems to me to be healthy enough to handle it."

The older woman's eyes slid away. Her lips worked as she struggled to withhold tears. She was silent for a few moments and then she whispered: "At home . . . at home, my home, a young man like Ralph would have servants waiting on him. He's so handsome, so like my father and brother in so many ways, but handsome like his father used to be." Her eyes focused at a distance. She was seeing something from her past.

"But . . ." Faith had much she wished to say but now she was uneasy about saying it. "It's you who needs the servants, I think," she said gently.

The woman gave her head a little shake. "I chose to give it up. It was my own choice." She sat back on her haunches awkwardly. "I fell in love, you see. Master

Keene was such a handsome young man. My family disapproved. They did not see that with his brilliance, his earnestness, his faith, he was better than all the others who courted me. We had to elope.''

''Ahhh . . .'' Faith did not know how to word what she wanted to ask. Finally she said, ''Does Master Keene also miss having servants?''

The gap-toothed grin spread across the other woman's face. ''Not he. He don't have much idea of what's going on around him. Not he. He's good at oratory and Bible reading and talking theology. You can't expect a man like that to pay attention to ordinary life.''

''No. No, indeed,'' agreed Faith feebly. Master Keene was a truly pious man, she realized — probably as bad as Papa. Uneasily she watched Mistress Keene's fumbling attempts to stir the dying coals. A ripple of alarm that chilled her more than the cold air ran through her. Surely Papa would clarify to this poor creature that she, at fifteen, could not be expected to take care of Papa and Peter, Master Keene and Ralph, the younger boys and, inevitably, this sick woman as well?

She spoke loudly: ''It is ridiculous for you to fix the fire when the men are here to do it, Mistress Keene.'' She stepped over to the ladder and called up, ''Ralph, Ralph? Your mother needs help.''

It wasn't Ralph who awoke to her call, but Papa — gray-faced and trembling. Her call had also awoken Master Keene, who peered at her from his pillows, his nightcap askew. ''Eh?'' He stared groggily at his wife and Faith.

Faith said calmly, ''Are you awake, Master Keene? Your wife is not well. I thought the boys, or perhaps you, could give her some assistance with the morning tasks.''

For the next few minutes, everyone was talking at once. Papa protested to Faith about ungratefulness. Mistress Keene protested that there was no reason at all she could not be serving her menfolk. Master Keene loudly asked what the problem was. The dog came to the door and barked.

Faith, resigned, went over to the hearth and started the fire. She looked around but could find no water for the kettle. She kept her back to Master Keene as she loudly asked his wife where she would find water. For answer she was handed two buckets and told how to reach the spring. It was a relief to escape the house.

When she first stepped from the door she was so full of resentment that she did not look about her. But she could not long ignore the peaceful beauty of the morning. Great pines towered overhead and majestic oaks glowed bronze with the coming of winter. By the time she had walked to the edge of the clearing the mists of resentment were rising from within her as surely as the mists of morning were rising in thin wisps from the clearing behind her.

She turned to look at the buildings she had been too tired to notice when she had entered the clearing at dusk. There were four houses in this settlement. None was large, but the one farthest up the hill was two stories high and had a small barn attached.

During the last few days Ralph had spoken often about the community. Three families in addition to the Keenes lived at High Hills. The Youngs, a middle-aged couple who had a little girl with them, lived in a large house. An elderly couple named Sedgewick lived in a small cabin. And a family named Brown lived in a house similar to the Keenes'. The big house uphill must be the one belonging to Goodman Young and his wife. She wondered where on the hill Papa would build their house and what it would look like.

Smoke curled from all four chimneys, so there must be others awake, but there was no one but herself outside. She turned to follow the path that led to the spring and stepped softly. It seemed sacrilege to break the peace of the morning.

A sound from behind spun her around to find Moses, the Keenes' large, shaggy black dog, directly behind her, wagging his tail so hard that his whole body shook. Faith reached out a tentative hand. Auntie Abbie had never kept a dog but the dogs in their village had often let her pat them. This large, shaggy creature pressed close, his trusting coffee-colored eyes watching her intelligently.

"Come, Moses."

He pranced ahead of her on the path and led the way, his tail wagging steadily. She followed him down to where the trees were so thick overhead that only a few rays of the morning sun filtered through. The brook flowing down from the spring splashed over the rocks. Every few feet it dropped a little lower and formed a pool. Some of the pools were as much as six feet wide, but the bed of the brook was cut deep into the rock of the hillside and narrowed in spots to but two feet wide.

The spring itself was a gush of water shooting out between two dark gray boulders. A solid, flattened log had been wedged below it to support buckets as they were filled. She drank before filling her buckets. Her cupped hands tingled from the icy cold.

Her buckets full, Faith set off for the house. Next time she would use the shoulder yoke that had been leaning against the wall near the door. She had not realized that two buckets of water could be so heavy.

Halfway back up the path she met an elderly man she vaguely remembered meeting the night before. Most of his face was hidden by a bushy white beard, but his pale blue eyes were alert and curious. "Miss Faith Ralston —that's your name, isn't it, young lady? Here, let me help you with those. What is Mistress Keene about, letting you carry heavy buckets when she has all those big slugabeds who could help you?"

This was so much in accord with her own opinion that Faith gave him a brilliant smile.

He grinned back, revealing even fewer teeth than Mistress Keene had.

"Ain't you a pretty sight for these old eyes? Now, you just hand those buckets to me, so, and we'll tell that lady a thing or two. Nice lady Mistress Keene is, but spoils them lads something awful. Thinks they be royal princes or some-at. Ain't good for 'em and so I'll tell her."

So he did as he staggered into the cabin with Faith's buckets.

"Oh, I never, Master Sedgewick, I never intended her to fill them buckets full."

"Shouldn't be filling them at all. Job of the lads to do heavy work like this. Don't want a lass this pretty to lose her bloom afore she's even bedded down," cackled the old fellow, pinching Faith's flaming cheeks.

This did nothing to placate Mistress Keene. "Nasty old gaffer," she hissed as his bent form departed. "Telling me what to do. Imagine!" She turned to Faith. "Nary a child, him and his goodwife. Barren, she is. But think they know it all when it comes to children!" A defiant snort ended this tirade as she turned to instruct Faith in the particular difficulties of cooking on her hearth.

By the time light flooded the one room of the house all were up. The younger boys were so lively and noisy that they seemed to fill all available space. The family ate the rough cornmeal porridge that Faith had watched Mistress Keene prepare. Faith wondered how she was to learn anything about cooking from Mistress Keene when the woman could not even produce an edible porridge.

Papa's grayness and shakiness had not left him and were so severe that it alarmed Faith. He was not even interested in contributing to the prayers at morning worship. She had assumed his weakness would leave him once the trip was completed. How old was Papa? Would he ever be able to build his house? What if—and her heart tightened with panic — what if he died, leaving her to the mercy of the Keenes?

She saw that Peter was watching Papa as closely as she was. Faith suddenly realized that Peter stood to lose more than she did if Papa died. At least she would have a role, unwelcome as it might be, with the Keenes. He would have nothing. As far as she knew, he owned nothing but the filthy clothing on his back.

Also, if Peter lost Papa he would lose someone he loved and respected. Peter never seemed to feel exasperated or annoyed with Papa as she did.

At the breakfast board Peter sat beside Ralph, his shoulders bent forward tensely, his long white fingers clenched. His thin nose quivered like a rabbit's. She watched as a large drop hanging from his nostrils got larger and larger. In the nick of time he bent his elbow up to his nose to wipe it. Peter's nose must have been dripping all his life. He almost never missed the timing of the twist of the elbow.

One might expect two boys so close in age as Peter and Ralph to have something in common, but they seemed not to. She looked curiously from one to the other. They did not even talk together.

Master Keene harrumphed and pronounced a final amen and Faith sat up. Worship had taken so long that the sun now illumined much more of the breakfast board. In the painful days ahead she guessed she would be counting the passing of every hour.

6 ❧ Misfortune

❧ Almost overnight the maple at the brow of the hill turned from green to gold. Faith had never seen so large a yellow tree. None of the trees in Sussex had glowed so brightly. Every time she stepped outside she stared at it in wonder.

She stepped outside often, for the men were working on the site for Papa's house and she took delight in every bit of progress they made. Papa had asked her to help choose from three possible sites and she had finally convinced him to choose the highest location. Their house would sit under the protective branches of a great oak. In summer the tree would shade them and in winter the leaves would fall and let the sun shine on the roof.

They had lived in High Hills for a week now and already Faith felt part of the little community. The men often worked together as they were this morning, for they accomplished difficult tasks more easily that way.

The women were more likely to work at home, but even so, Faith was getting to know them. She loved the shy, elderly Mistress Sedgewick who spent long hours knitting. She was amazed and almost overwhelmed by Mistress Brown, an energetic woman who controlled her lively sons by bellowing at them and chopped wood alongside her husband. Her favorite was Goodwife Young, a tranquil woman who had often been quietly helpful to her.

Now that the heavy chores of the morning were done, Faith sat on the bench by the back door with half her attention on the worksite and half on the mending she was doing. Papa was busy with the light chopping, for he was neither strong enough nor skilled enough to handle a large ax safely. Peter, to her surprise, was better at chopping down trees than most of the men. Caleb and Hosea, the Keene twins, found Peter's long white face a good subject for ridicule, but no one could jeer at the way he wielded an ax. He had been trained in carpentry, Papa said, and was skillful with any aspect of handling wood.

A scream from the worksite made her leap up to see what was wrong. Was it an animal who had been injured or was it one of the men? From where she stood she could see that the men were in a circle around someone and Peter — was it Peter? — was bending over.

"Faith!" That was Ralph, yelling and beckoning.

Faith felt as if she were flying up the hill. It was like being in a bad dream where she would run and run and yet cover no ground. Finally she was there and old Master Sedgewick stepped in front of her.

"No need for you to be here. Menfolk can take care of this problem, Miss Faith. Your pa's had a slip of the ax. Best you go down and tell Mistress Keene to rip up a few bandages. We'll bring him down in a minute and that's what he'll be needing."

She pushed him aside. Papa was lying down with a great gash at the side of his leg. Blood had spurted out all over everything, especially over Peter who was trying to hold the wound shut. Everyone else seemed paralyzed and helpless.

Papa's face was drawn tight. The skin gleamed pale over his bony cheeks and scalp. She thought he had fainted until his eyelids flickered and he gazed directly at her, his large bloodshot eyes revealing the anguish his clenched jaws kept him from expressing.

For a moment vomit came up into her mouth and she felt cold, but a memory of Auntie Abbie standing over her aged gardener and scolding while she bandaged him up sustained her. Not for nothing had Faith trailed after Auntie Abbie. Old Clem's accident had been very similar.

"Don't move him," ordered Faith. "Ralph, go down and get some bandages from your ma."

She reached down and pulled the hem off her apron. While Peter held the edges of the wound together as tightly as he could she tied her bandage around Papa's leg, knotting it fast. Again and again she ripped from the worn apron, and again and again she knotted her bandages around. Before long the blood had ceased to flow and instead seeped slowly.

"That was very neatly done, Faith," said Master Keene. "I would have done it myself if I'd had an apron."

"Anything will do — even a shirt," said Faith, more sharply than was perhaps seemly. "That is, of course, if you don't have an apron handy."

"He's going to be casting his oats," announced Master Sedgewick interestedly.

Faith turned to Papa quickly. "Oh, Papa, you mustn't move! Don't be sick!"

He did not look up at her but he managed to avoid vomiting.

"He must stay still, you're right about that, Miss Faith," said Goodman Young. "Don't move, sir. We'll move you in a few minutes, but you ought to lie still a bit first."

Papa lay on the cold ground while the men argued among themselves, finally deciding he would best be carried atop a door. If they moved slowly the bleeding should not worsen. Faith stepped back, glad to be ignored, for now that the moment of crisis had passed she felt weak and could not bring herself to look again at the bloodstained bandages she had tied around Papa's leg.

The men finally settled how to move Papa onto the door and carried him, with much warning and complaint to one another, down the rocky slope. Faith trailed after them. She knew she had ceased disliking Papa so much, but she had never before felt this fierce, protective fondness for him. She knew that now she would do everything in her power to help him. She and Papa desperately needed each other in this frightening wilderness.

Much to her surprise, Mistress Keene handled the emergency with brisk efficiency. "Oh my, oh my," she clucked as she bustled about. "And to think he be having something like this and him just beginning to work. Oh, lordy be." She pulled blankets tight around his shoulders, tucked two pillows under Papa's head, and shooed the men out. "We women don't need you no more. Off with you now."

Goodwife Young, sensible as usual, stepped in to join them. She looked over Papa's leg and then put her arm around Faith and gave her a little hug. "Don't worry," she said. "Mistress Keene has taught us all a lot about treating illness and injury. Your pa's in good hands."

"We can use your help, Susan," said Mistress Keene, "but lordy be, don't let Mistress Sedgewick or Hattie Brown in here. Got enough on our hands without the flutterin's of the one and the knocking about of the other. I declare, Hattie thumps around inside as bad as a horse would.

"Comfrey, that's what we want now," said Mistress Keene as she poked through her supplies. "Lots of it I set aside this summer. Make a tea of it, we will, and wash off the wound with more. Then we'll soak a bandage in some more comfrey and fresh wrap it. Then another bandage over that. Clean bandages, that's what we want. Some says to use up old dirty rags on bloody stuff so's you can throw them out. Not me. I use clean, I do. Been doing it for years. Always had good healing in this family.''

Faith cleared her throat. ''My auntie believed in clean bandages too,'' she agreed, her voice rough.

''Tisanes within, lotions without, I say,'' announced Mistress Keene proudly. ''Watch how I do this.''

She was so brisk, so happily efficient, that Faith found it difficult to think of her as the same woman who had dragged around ineffectively these last few days. The tisane made, Mistress Keene had Faith give some to Papa while she boiled the bandages in the pot with the rest.

Papa was pale and trembling. He tried to wave the cup away but Faith was persistent. ''You really must have it, Papa. I truly think it is good for you.'' Goodwife Young took the cup and approached him so firmly that, with a sigh, he gave in and slowly drank it down. Beads of cold sweat stood out on his forehead and dark circles of pain rimmed his eyes.

After he swallowed the last drop he whispered, ''Faith, my child, if I die from this wound, I commend you to marry Peter. He is a responsible lad and will build your house for you.''

''Well, I never!'' exclaimed Mistress Keene as she started cutting away the bandages that Faith had tied on. ''As if you would die from such a wound as this! I'm a better nurse than that, I'll have you know. And should anything happen to leave Faith without a father, Master Ralston, let me tell you she'd be better off marrying my

Ralph. She could keep on living right here in this house
and have a family of her own, so she could.''

Papa frowned, so annoyed he scarcely noticed the
tugging at his leg. ''It is the obligation of the parent,
Mistress Keene, to make provision for the child and I
have — *ow*!''

''See there? You're just upsetting yourself unneces-
sarily, Master Ralston. Stay still and keep quiet and I'll
be done in no time.''

By the time she finished firmly tying the last strip of
bandage, Papa was gasping for breath. He lay back
against the pillows utterly exhausted. Faith took one look
at his drawn face and then averted her gaze as she and
Goodwife Young followed Mistress Keene's instructions, wrapping him warmly.

After he was wrapped in his blanket, Mistress Keene
put warmed soapstones around him and then piled blanket after blanket from the other beds over him. ''Good
thing it ain't night so that other folks be needing them,''
she said to Faith. ''After accidents folks sometimes get
real cold. It ain't good for them and you have to work
hard to keep them warm. If we didn't have blankets I'd
bring in Moses and have him lay close to your pa.''

Faith was relieved there were enough blankets. Papa
was not as fond of dogs as she was and he already had
a lot of swollen lumps from the bites of Moses's fleas.

Goodwife Young left to handle her own chores and
Mistress Keene left Faith in charge of Papa. By evening,
when the men broke off working on the house site, Papa
was still sleeping. Master Sedgewick and the other men

stopped by the door to find out how he was doing. Master Sedgewick whispered loudly to Faith, ''That young man of your'n, he be right good at chopping. He'll take over for your pa just fine. Keep your pa in bed now. He ain't such a great worker. We work better without having him underfoot, I tell you. I guess you'd call him a brain worker.''

Ralph gave a short laugh as he walked by. Faith did not mind the criticism of Papa from Master Sedgewick, but she resented it fiercely from Ralph. ''He tries. He tries hard,'' she said angrily.

''Yes, yes, Miss Faith, never you mind,'' Master Sedgewick said as he patted her arm. Ralph just shrugged.

Supper was an awkward meal with Papa sleeping just across the room and the family trying not to make noise that would awaken him.

''I don't think we ought to do any more work on the site,'' said Ralph after they had been eating for a while. ''After all, he can live here with us when Faith and I are married.''

Caleb giggled and Faith almost choked in her astonishment. Ralph was giving her a wickedly slanted look and at her astonished gaze he grinned. ''That is what will happen, don't you think, Faith?''

She suddenly blushed so hot that her skin itched. ''It's mean of you to tease me this way,'' she said angrily.

''Oh, come, girl,'' began Master Keene, smiling on his oldest son. ''A girl doesn't do well to receive the attentions of a young man so ungraciously.''

Faith thumped her bowl on the table. ''Then the young

man ought to be gracious in his attentions. I have no expectation of marrying Ralph. Papa wants me to marry Peter.''

Now it was Peter's turn to be aghast, which he definitely was. He stared at Faith and his Adam's apple slid up and down as he swallowed convulsively.

Ralph gave him a superior sneer before saying to Faith, "Even your Papa will give you some choice, I think.''

Faith glared. "I choose not to marry at all. My Auntie Abbie thinks I'm too young. She wants me to wait until I'm older.''

Peter began to breathe again. Ralph gave one of his shrugs. "You're old enough.''

"Maybe," granted Faith. "At home it was different. I'm going to wait.''

Papa stirred in his sleep and groaned. Glad of an excuse to leave the table, Faith hurried across to him. His head was burning with fever. When he looked up he did not at first recognize her, then mumbled something she could not understand.

"It's going to be a bad night," said Mistress Keene. She leaned over the bed and pulled off the top blankets.

"What can I do for him?" Faith tried not to let the panic sound in her voice.

"Now he's got the fever we'll take some of the blankets off. Won't do to let him get cold though. You'll have to stay by him for the night. Cold cloths to the head and don't let him kick off all the blankets or rip off the bandages.''

These instructions were not easy to follow. After sunset the family went to bed, leaving the fire glowing for warmth and light. Faith stayed beside the bed trying to calm Papa when he muttered and tried to climb out of bed. The night seemed endless. When Papa was quiet she would start to nod, only to be wakened a moment later by his muttering.

In the middle of the night there came a scratch at the door and Faith let Moses enter, grateful for his company. The furry body of the dog pressed against her. He wagged his tail whenever she looked down at him and his large eyes seemed sympathetic. Even Papa seemed to calm somewhat with his presence, as if the rhythmical thwacking of Moses's tail on the floor was reassuring to him also.

Toward morning Papa settled into a normal sleep. Faith threw the last of the wood onto the fire and lay down before it with her head on Moses's broad back. The first bleak rays of morning sun penetrated the house just as she closed her eyes.

7 ~ Massacre

~ "Go ahead, go ahead. Go nutting while you can and I'll sit here and churn for you. At least it is one useful thing I can do." Papa swatted at Faith with his makeshift cane and she quickly left the stool by the butter churn.

It had been a week since his accident and he was much better. She and Papa and Peter had been in High Hills for two weeks now and were all learning new skills. Certainly Papa had never churned butter before.

"All right, Betty, I will get a basket or two and be with you right away," Faith told the child who was patiently waiting. Faith went inside, leaving Betty and Papa to watch the men working on the hill at the house site.

"Papa will churn for me," Faith explained to Mistress Keene. "It will give him something to do and I'll be able to go with little Betty Young to gather pignuts. Do you have a basket I may use?"

"Pignuts?" Mistress Keene slowed her spinning wheel and frowned at Faith. "Small they are, hardly worth the bother. I don't care for any variety of hickory nut myself. I never send the boys after them." Faith refrained from saying that she hardly ever sent the boys after anything. "Most folks feed them to the hogs. Ah, well, we don't have any other nuts put aside for winter, and even if small, they are filling."

She waved her hand toward the baskets hanging on the wall near the door. Faith took two. She knew Papa would insist she give some of the nuts to the Keenes, but she also intended to collect enough for Papa's household-to-be. After all, Goodman Young had said that he thought the men could do enough work on Papa's house so that she and Papa and Peter could move in before heavy winter came.

Betty set off down the path, bouncing and skipping. She was certainly a cheerful child considering her background. Goodwife Young said her husband had found Betty beside the body of her dead mother in a cabin outside Springfield and had taken her home. They didn't even know what her last name was. The Youngs had been raising her for three years now and treated her as if she were their own. Betty, being the youngest child at High Hills, was favored by everyone.

Moses, who had been curled up beside Papa, leapt up and followed on her heels. Faith brought up the rear. She looked back once to watch Papa as he struggled to get the rhythm of churning and then turned to the path, relieved to have a break from the chores. Faith followed

Betty down along the path by the spring. They jumped over the brook at the floor of the ravine and climbed up the steep far side. As they went up, the sun shone down on them through the golden leaves of the maples on the ridge. Many of the brilliant fall colors were passing, but Faith thought the soft browns and grays were almost more beautiful.

They clambered up and over the ridge and were out of sight of the settlement when Betty pointed to branches overhead. "There, those are the nuts." Then she looked around at the thick layer of nuts on the woodland floor. "We won't be able to get them all today," she said, pleased. "Happen we'll have to come back again." She knelt and industriously started picking fallen nuts from the ground.

For a moment Faith simply stood and soaked in the beauty of the afternoon. The sun glinted on the scarlet of the sumac next to them. The sounds of the men working at the house site echoed across the ravine. The nearby stand of laurel rustled in the afternoon breeze. It was a moment of utter peace.

Suddenly Moses threw back his head and howled. The oddly mournful sound made Faith nervous. She was glad to see him trot back to the settlement. She knelt to fill her baskets. The first basket filled rapidly and she was just beginning to fill the second one when there came an anguished high-pitched howl from Moses. A shiver ran down her back and she ran over to look down the path to the settlement.

Betty came to stand beside Faith. "Was that Moses?"

"Betty, I don't see him, but I think it was. He must have been hurt somehow."

"I want to go home now," complained Betty a bit peevishly.

"I do too. I can't imagine . . . but if he's hurt, surely someone will tend to him. I should finish filling my baskets." She sighed impatiently. "You may start ahead, Betty. I'll keep a watch on you until you top the rise of the path by the spring. Then you'll be in view of the houses so you won't need me to watch you. I'll be right along."

"All right."

Now Faith gathered her nuts rapidly. Silly to be so concerned for the dog. Probably nothing very much was wrong and if it were, someone was there to care for him. Still, she did want to get back to reassure herself. She stood again to watch as Betty's blue-frocked figure topped the rise beyond the spring. Out of the corner of her eye she saw something move down by the brook. The laurel stirred. Something — or someone — was crawling through it. Whatever it was, she thought she had better race back to the clearing.

She could not dash off with a large basket on each arm. Keeping her eyes steadily on the laurel, she felt behind on the ground for the little hole she had seen near the roots of a hickory. She scooped away the leaves, set her two baskets in the pocket, and spread leaves over them. Now she could come back and get them when she had someone with her.

She crouched and darted a quick glance around, ready to run, when she heard a faint groan. Then a whimper. Surely it wasn't Moses! Of course, if he was hurt and no one had yet helped him, this is just what he might do — slink away to hide in an impenetrable stand of bushes. She waited and was rewarded by a second whimper.

Her call was soft, but it was enough. An eager whine answered her. She hurried around to the side of the laurel where she had seen movement and peeked in. The dog was not to be seen, but there were broken branches here. She wriggled flat and crept inside as best she could.

Moses had burrowed well into the middle of a stand of laurel. It was so thick that it was almost dark inside where she found him. He looked at her with mournful eyes. She examined him all over to find where he was injured. His head was fine and, although it was difficult to see them all, his paws seemed fine also. Finally she saw the arrow sticking out of the dog's back.

Terror washed over her, blocking out thought and common sense. She did not even let herself think about what an arrow meant, so she did not consider what she might do for her own safety or the safety of the others. Instead, she concentrated all her attention on the arrow and how she might get it out.

With shaking fingers she felt around the dog's flank, trying to figure out how deeply the point was embedded, trying to see how she might best extract it. Already there was a lot of blood loss. Evidently the arrow had knocked against branches as the dog crawled in to hide. The point must be in deeply or it would have been knocked out by now.

If she leaned over and pulled, it was inevitable that the dog would bite her. Struggling and twisting, she moved over his body so that she faced his tail end instead of his mouth. She pressed against the branches behind her, breaking them until she found a spot where she could move to brace both of her arms over him. She drew a deep breath to steady herself, took hold of the arrow and pulled up as firmly and quickly as she could. It held at first and the dog started writhing. Before he could twist enough to cause himself more damage, he gave a ghastly sound and the arrow slid out, followed by a great well of blood.

The dog was whimpering now. Faith joined him, unaware of the noise she was making. For the second time she pulled off her apron to staunch a wound. This time there wasn't an opportunity to bandage properly. Instead, she wadded up the fabric and pressed it down as firmly as she could to prevent the incessant flow of blood. How long could the poor animal bleed before he died?

When the flow of blood eased, her breathing, although still ragged, began to calm until she began to more fully consider the significance of the arrow in the dog's back. Certainly it had been an Indian who shot the arrow, but where had it come from? When Moses howled, it sounded like he had been in the woods above the house site at which the men were working.

There were no sounds coming from there now. She

and Moses were in a cocoon within the laurel, surrounded by an eerie silence. Faith caught her breath and
strained to listen. Even in his pain the dog realized she
was waiting for something. The girl and dog stared at
each other. The silence strung out until Faith's chest
hurt with the tension.

Then it came as she had known it would — the
screaming she had been told so much about — the war
cries of the Indians! The sounds echoed across the ravine
and re-echoed, freezing the blood in her veins. She felt
sick and faint and the sounds seemed to resound in a
vast cavern at the top of her head.

She pressed her hands hard over her ears and flung
herself on top of the dog. They were both shuddering,
cold with terror. A while later — she did not know how
long — she was vaguely aware she had fainted. With
returning consciousness she heard other sounds in among
the war cries. Voices carried well across the ravine.
There were shouts of rage, confused orders, screams of
agony. A lull in the noise framed all too sharply one
thin, high-pitched wail, much like the cry of a child —
a child that could be Betty. Again Faith fainted.

The sharpness of the laurel, thick and brittle, brought
her back to consciousness. Moses was licking her face.
Faith lifted her head and listened. Nothing. She waited.

She heard the crackle and roar at about the same time
that she smelled the burning wood. She vaguely realized
she should plan what to do next, but her frightened mind
would not function. She wanted desperately to go out,
to see if anyone needed her. What if Papa could be

saved by something she could do? Would they all be dead? Perhaps no one was. Perhaps they had all been kidnapped to be taken to Canada. Echoing through her fear was a memory of Ralph telling of a settlement where everyone had been taken to Canada. She liked that idea. That might have happened!

She drifted into sleep. But because of cold and bad dreams, the sleep came only in snatches. Only the part of her next to Moses had any warmth. There was little room for them here. The laurel cut into her with every motion she made. The pain from it had a certain rightness and she welcomed it. It was the one definite feeling that was acceptable. Her head felt very light. Through the night she drifted continuously in and out of sleep. There was one recurring nightmare — of Auntie Abbie, wounded and screaming in a burning house awaiting rescue by Faith, who was tied hand and foot. Her waking thoughts were even worse. Moses remained immobile but she thought he must be alive because he was still warm. The night seemed to go on for an eternity.

With the first rays of morning light she was unable to sleep any more. She still shook, now as much from cold as from fear. Her numbed mind slowly grappled with a few thoughts. Was it safe to leave the laurel? Should she run farther into the woods? Was it possible to live alone in the woods? Would she be able to help anyone if she went back to the settlement? Maybe there was an injured person she could nurse. Maybe she need not be all alone.

Maybe if she went back she wouldn't find things as

bad as she was imagining them. All those horrible tales that Ralph had told — maybe she was thinking the worst because of them.

The sun moved up above the horizon. It was now beyond the usual time for breakfast. Slowly, painfully, carefully, she eased herself away from the large dog and crept backward.

Just as she was about to push out of the laurel she froze. Those were footsteps outside. Someone was coming along the ridge of the hill above her and was moving with slow, cautious footsteps. The steps became careless, staggering; the walker seemed to have abandoned caution. The walker lost footing. She heard the fall, the body sliding down toward the stream. Silence.

Why had there been no cry? Had it been an Indian or a settler? Surely those feet had been shod in boots. She waited.

By high noon the warmth of the sun penetrated even into the laurel. Faith's muscles had begun to cramp so badly that she did not notice. A nudge against her face made her aware that Moses wanted to get out. Somehow he had managed to pull his body around and she was now in his way. He would not be able to leave until she did. His wounded body would never be able to push through the heavy growth around them.

And why shouldn't she go out? What difference did it make now? She would surely die of thirst or hunger if she did not move from where she was. If Indians kidnapped her, at least they might feed her. And if they killed her she would just be dead, just as she would be if she continued to hide in the laurel. And anyway, Moses would know enough not to go out if there were Indians, wouldn't he? Wouldn't he be able to smell them?

Slowly, painfully, she backed out. Between tension and inactivity her muscles were jumping and cramping. The bright sunlight hurt her eyes and it took time to adjust. She stood, staggered, and almost fell. Moses lurched out behind her and collapsed. She leaned over to help hoist him onto his feet and his eyes were blank with pain. His nose, the whole top of his head, were hot to the touch.

Moses would need water. Papa had been very thirsty when he lost all that blood after his accident. The thought of water brought her own thirst to awareness. Moses pulled himself to his feet, almost lost his balance, and moved again. Awkwardly she clasped her hands around his chest and urged him forward. Step by graceless step they moved down the side of the ravine. She abandoned any hope of moving cautiously. The only thing of importance now was to get to the brook with Moses.

8 ❧ *Alone*

❧ In the sun-warmed air of the afternoon the smell of the dying fire drifted across the ravine. If it were not for that odor, Faith could almost pretend nothing had happened. She wished she could tell herself it had been a bad dream. Or maybe, she thought, there was something wrong with her mind — and her sense of smell. It seemed bizarre that the air was filled with such a terrible odor when, standing at the edge of the ravine, well out of sight of the clearing, she looked upon a scene of brilliant fall beauty. Around her were glowing yellow maples, a pink and orange maple, and deep russet oaks. Below was a stand of scarlet sumac. The grass by the sumac had been pressed down. That must be the spot where the body that she had heard had slid down.

 The earth seemed to tilt, jolting her again into a state close to paralysis from terror — a feeling that was now becoming familiar. The altered feeling in her head ticked off a memory from childhood of a body swinging from a gibbet, Auntie Abbie's firm clasp on her small hand, and Auntie's crisp voice saying, "No need for you to be sick, Faith. Looks bad and smells bad, it's true, but he's dead. He gets no good out of your feeling bad." The small Faith had shrunk away and turned her head. Auntie Abbie had lifted her chin. "Keep your back straight when you face unpleasant things, child. Oak trees stand straight and tall in all sorts of weather. You don't want to flop over like a squash."

Faith drew a deep breath and straightened her shoulders. She looked about, almost expecting to see Auntie.

Moses started to lurch forward again. Faith laced her fingers under his broad chest and propped him upright. Slowly, awkwardly, staggering and resting, the girl and dog continued their way down toward the stream.

They passed the stand of sumac and came upon the boots she had heard. The dog sniffed them disinterestedly. Then he pulled free of her clutching fingers and lowered himself to drink. Faith's eyes traveled slowly from the boots along to the deerskin breeches, to the stained and ripped shirt. The head lay in the water.

Suddenly frantic, she pulled and dragged the leaden body, moving it sideways, rolling it over. She should have recognized him by the clothing, but until she saw the contorted grimace on the stiffened face, she had not identified him as Ralph.

The top of his scalp was gone. That accounted for all the blood on his shirt. She wondered how he had escaped after that. She wondered how he had lived through the night. But all her wondering was done in a far corner of her brain while she clung to a branch and retched repeatedly.

She was weak and trembling by the time she stopped. The dry retching left her throat feeling as if it had been ripped apart. She stared blindly at Moses as he stood in the water lapping noisily, completely ignoring the body. She stumbled into the stream beside him. She knelt in the water and dipped her face. The cold of the water came as a shock. She scooped water into her cupped hands and drank. Settling near her in the clear pool of water was a dark substance that looked like clotted blood. She stirred the water with her hand and it disappeared.

Faith sat back on her haunches and struggled to think. Her brain would not focus. She felt dazed. She frowned as she tried to shake her confusion.

She drank again, then pulled herself upright and walked to the far bank of the stream, her wet shoes and skirts dragging at her ankles, weighing down her feet. The cold stream had done more than just slake her thirst; it had also helped to sharpen her wits. Now she was aware that she was hungry.

Moses, too, must be hungry. He lumbered across the stream and pressed against her before he began the climb up the side of the ravine to the clearing. Because she did not want to see the scene she would come upon in the clearing, she followed the dog reluctantly. Come what may, she had no intention of being left alone with the body in the stream.

Moses had difficulty moving up the steep path and she often had to shove him along. There weren't many woodland sounds this afternoon. The stench of the fire had driven most living creatures into the forest. Faith heard only one bird, a jay in the distance that called continuously.

Usually as she topped the rise she was able to see all four houses of the community. Now none was standing. The buildings that had belonged to the Keenes, the Sedgewicks, and the Browns were charred rubble. Goodman Young's house still had part of one back wall standing. Smoke rose lazily from the depths of the tumbled, blackened remains. Here above the ravine the stench was much worse.

Household supplies littered the ground. As Faith came closer a vulture rose with a noisy flapping of wings and circled overhead. Faith stepped over a wooden trencher and a candlestick before coming upon a pile of rags. From the rags an arm stretched out in her direction, and on the other side she saw legs. The tilting feeling came again. Faith tried to breathe slowly and remembered the words of Auntie Abbie: ''An oak tree stands tall.'' She cringed, then steeled herself and went closer. As badly bloodied and battered as the body was, it was still identifiable as Master Keene. He was the only man to have worn a bright blue coat.

The sick feeling was not as bad this time as it had been when she had seen Ralph. She was soon able to walk around the corpse and go on to the remains of the Keene cabin. Papa's body lay near the doorstep. A tomahawk had severed his scalp in two. A swarm of flies buzzed around his remains. Wave after wave of cold passed through her, so intense that her skin crawled and her teeth ached.

She twisted her head from side to side. With the cold came faintness. The buzzing of flies rose louder and louder. Moses nudged her. Slowly the faintness receded, but the cold remained. She twisted her head away; she would not look at Papa again. She backed up and walked far around his body.

Where were the others? As she scanned the clearing she glimpsed a flicker of white beyond the Sedgewicks' cellar hole. Moses saw it also and began to stagger uphill. Halfway up he was distracted by another body. Looking down at the clothing, she thought it was Master Sedgewick. She could not make herself roll the body over to see the face.

Now, with three men found, it seemed very important to locate every body possible. She walked back and forth across the settlement until she located the body of every adult male except Peter. Each had been tomahawked— none was easy to recognize.

By the end of this search her eyes felt dry and gritty. She moved jerkily, in puppet fashion. Her eyes kept scanning the scene but she did not register what she was seeing. When the dog moved, she moved. When the dog stopped, she stopped and waited, staring blankly about.

Somewhere in the distance someone seemed to be repeating words she had heard before. "My God, my

God, why hast thou forsaken me?'' She was confused.
Was someone speaking in the wind or were those words
she had read somewhere?

This continued until Moses burrowed his head behind
a log near the Sedgewick cellar hole and came up with
a loaf of bread. Faith felt the sharp, twisting pain of
hunger and grabbed for the loaf. Moses backed away
growling, but when she fiercely began to pry it from his
jowls, he released it.

The bread was very hard and partially burnt. She
broke it in two, presented one half to the dog, and began
a frenzied gnawing on the other. Forgetting all else, she
plumped herself down on the ground beside Moses and
ate until the last crumb was gone. Not until she licked
her fingers did she again become aware of her surround-
ings, the stench, and the swarms of flies. The words she
had heard before came back and seemed to hover, almost
visibly, in the clearing.

A dark cloud passed overhead and a smattering of
raindrops hissed on the still hot coals. The accompanying chill wind reminded her of the cold night she had
passed. Another night was on its way and she had no
protection. She needed more food and she needed a place
to sleep.

Faith began an aimless wandering over the devastated
area. When she tripped over a bottle it occurred to
her that she ought to scan the ground for every item
that might help her survive. The bottle, a wooden
trencher, a single shoe, a silver cup, a length of ragged
toweling — little enough remained intact, but those

things that did went into her upheld skirt. Passing yet again near Master Sedgewick's body she recalled that he had usually carried a knife thrust through his belt. She searched out a long, sturdy stick and, using it as a lever, slowly raised the old man's body. Yes, the knife was there. He had fallen on it, else surely the Indians would have taken it. She took a deep breath, reached down, and tugged the knife from its sheath.

Somehow, doing this made her feel better. He would have wanted her to have the knife; he had been a generous man and had been kindly to her.

Finally she remembered the root cellar. Goodman Brown had told her of it one morning when they had been walking up to Papa's house site. Pleased by her interest, he had shown it to her. "I tried to talk your pa into digging one, Miss Faith," he said. "However, he don't think it is important. Master Keene doesn't have one, you know. I find it of greatest importance. Keeps stored foods from freezing in the winter and spoiling in the summer. All my harvest is in here."

Now she tried to picture where Goodman Brown and she had stood as they talked. The ground around the houses had changed from the fighting and the fire. She remembered that a heavy layer of moss had been placed over the door to the root cellar to protect it from the weather as well as to hide it. Perhaps one of the women or children had thought to hide in it!

Hope sharpened her memory. The door had been to the left of a large outcropping of rock. She located the rock and felt on the ground for the large metal ring.

Before lifting it she looked around carefully. Indians might still be lingering in the area. As she looked about, she again noticed the flicker of white, now on the hill beyond the new house site.

Caution made her decide to identify that whiteness before opening the cellar door. A root cellar might be a great place to hide; it might also be a place to be trapped. Moses had collapsed after eating. He whined when she left him, but she knew she must find out what was up on the hill.

She clambered over the mossy embankment just below the site of Papa's house. It was just beyond this clearing, where the men had been cutting wood, that she had seen the white. She tripped over an adz lying on the ground. She was bending over to pick it up when the flash of white became large and pushed through the shrubbery. "*Baaaaa*," bleated Blanche, Goodman Young's goat. The goat trotted forward, shoved her nose against Faith's arm, and baaed again.

Faith opened her mouth to say the goat's name, but she could not mouth the word. It frightened her that she could make only an almost soundless, unintelligible garbling. But she patted the goat and hugged it, tears running down her cheeks.

After the first flush of excitement she looked down and felt the goat's udder. It was full of milk. Without moving from the spot the girl tried to milk the goat, aiming the milk into the silver cup she had found and now carried in her skirt. Faith was inexperienced in milking and the goat was painfully full. Between the two of them they managed to get milk all over the ground before any flowed into the cup. Faith struggled along, drinking up the milk as soon as the cup held enough for a swallow. She was going to have to find a bucket somewhere so that she could use both hands and milk the goat properly, according to the method Goodman Young had showed her.

Satisfied at last, Faith returned with the goat to the dog, who was still lying beside the root cellar door. It was a heavy door, built to withstand winter weather. Faith's fingers were bruised before she managed to pull it open. The cellar was dark inside and smelled musty. She peered into the darkness for some time before she dared to step down. As soon as she moved fully inside, the doorway darkened. She turned in fear, but the two heads that blocked out the light were those of the goat and the dog.

There was grain and wheat in quantity, but as she had no way of grinding them, they were useless to her. In addition there were squashes and onions, dried chevon and some semisoft cheese. Even the squash would take cooking and she did not want to set a fire. She struggled back out of the cellar, the cheese hugged to her chest.

She had thought fleetingly that the root cellar might be a place for her to sleep, but the dog might not be able to get out once he was in, and she was sure it would be awkward for Blanche. To sleep without them by her side was unthinkable. Besides, it was damp in the cellar. She wondered why the wheat did not mold.

She recalled the Keene twins talking about a secret

cave. She had the impression it was somewhere near the stream. If it was a real cave, perhaps it would provide protection for the night. Anyplace would be better than this site of desolation and horror, a place that even God had abandoned. Without looking behind, Faith set off for the ravine, the goat at one side and the dog at the other.

9 ✒ The Cave

✒   Maybe there was no cave along the ravine. Maybe
Caleb and Hosea had been lying when they told her
about it. Faith stood on the path near the spring and
looked around hopelessly. For more than two hours
she climbed up and slid down the sides of the ravine
searching for the cave. No one but themselves knew
of it, the twins had said. That is why they would not
show it to her.

Maybe she was looking in the wrong place. She walked
down to a spot on the path below a great oak. A pile
of boulders, loosened from somewhere higher along the
side of the ravine, lay heaped at the high side of the
path. Maybe the spot from which these boulders had
come was now a cave. Blanche, who had been eating
grass at the edge of the path, climbed over and around
the boulders and then headed diagonally up the side of
the ravine as if she had a goal in mind. Maybe the goat

had followed the twins to the cave at some time. Faith decided to follow her. Behind them on the path Moses started moaning mournfully.

The goat scampered over the rocks. Faith followed, slipping awkwardly on the moss-covered rocks. Soon she began to pick up the faint signs of the trail. Blanche had almost reached the top of the ravine when suddenly she disappeared. Faith doggedly continued upward until the trail ended on a rock shelf hidden behind a thick growth of saplings. The shelf dipped backward toward the ravine wall where a heavy fall of vines was still swinging from the passage of the goat. Faith pushed the vines aside and found a shallow entry. Blanche's yellow eyes blinked at the sudden light and then she jumped out and was on her way back down the path.

Faith ducked her head under the vines and entered the cave, careful not to rip its green curtain. It was not a big cave, but was much larger than she had expected. It was actually only a nook at the side of the ravine with an overhang of growth, which, while it hid the cave from view, would not be altogether successful for blocking out rain. There was space to stand and enough room for herself, Blanche, and Moses to sleep there if they crowded together.

Items that the Keene twins had collected were stacked on a rock outcropping at the rear of the cave. Papa's Bible! How had they had the boldness to steal that? They must have taken it after he became ill. And Papa's coin box — those wicked boys! A rusted flint box held a silver ring and two gold pieces. From whom had those come? If she lived much longer she supposed these things might be useful.

She unknotted her skirt and carefully deposited the items she had collected. They all smelled of the fire. Before she set the knife down she ran her finger down the sharp blade. Would she have the courage to use it on an Indian if she needed to protect herself? Her lips tightened. More likely the time would come when she would need to use it on herself. She smiled bitterly. Only a few days ago that idea would have been unthinkable.

Already it was getting dark. She broke off a hunk of the cheese, thought of Moses and broke off another hunk. Blanche had already bounded back down to the path and could be heard at the spring. Faith made her way down to the unhappy dog and began to lead him back up to the cave.

Moses seemed especially wary now. It took all her energy to encourage him to struggle along the path and then up over the rocks to the cave. Once there he flopped down against the innermost wall and immediately went to sleep.

Faith knew that she would not be able to sleep unless the goat was inside the cave with her, too. She tugged Blanche by the wattles until the reluctant creature finally came inside. There the goat settled down docilely next to the opening.

Faith lay down between the two animals but her muscles were too tight for her to find a comfortable position. Dusk passed into dark. She gave up trying to sleep and sat up. She yanked the goat a little closer to the center of the cave and sat upright near the vines that hung over it. At long last the goat lay down again. Faith dozed off and on as she sat.

In the deep of the night she awoke. The sound of screams came from the upper edge of the ravine, above their heads. Scream after scream rose through the cold night air to end in a quivering crescendo. If all the fiends of hell had let loose at once they could sound no worse. The goat leapt to her feet, trembling violently. At first Faith thought her heart had stopped. She tried to block the sound from her ears and rocked back and forth in terror.

At least these screams were not from human throats. She had heard this sound once before when wildcats invaded the settlement, drawn by the scent of an injured goat. Attracted to the smell of blood, the Keenes had said. Were they drawn now by the smell of Moses or were they after the bodies in the clearing? The awful thought that they might feast on the remains of the dead men made her bite down on her knuckles to keep from screaming back at them.

The wildcats apparently caught some of the odors from the cave, for they came and screamed closely over-head. Every few minutes the screams grew muted as they returned to the site of the fire, but then they would return to the edge of the ravine. Faith guessed that there were eight or ten of them. She stood and felt carefully on the ledge for the knife she had placed there. Then she knelt, facing the opening. She did not think she could fight a wildcat with a knife, but if one tried to get into the cave she was certainly going to try.

She had no way of telling how long the wildcats screamed. It might have been minutes; it seemed like hours. When Faith finally dozed off again, the screams were fading into the distance. Her feet had gone to sleep and her hand was so tightly clenched around the knife that she could not release it.

At dawn Faith struggled free from the horrors in her dreams to find herself lying with her feet at the front of the cave and her head on top of Moses. Her whole body ached and the air was chill. Blanche stood and snorted as Faith sat up, but the dog remained motionless. Poor Moses! He needed every bit of sleep he could get. She carefully avoided waking him.

Blanche stumbled over Moses and pushed in her eagerness to get out. Faith drew a deep breath and, reaching out, pulled up the vines to let in the light of day.

10 ❧ Morning

❧ Blanche brushed by Faith and clambered down the rocks to the trail. Faith stepped out slowly. The sun had scarcely begun to rise and the ground was wet with dew; the slanting rays of the sun caught on the threads of spiders and sparkled on the dewdrops that clung to them. She stretched out her arms, easing the tightness in her muscles. There was still no birdsong. She felt, for that moment, as if she were the only creature alive.

A wave of desolation engulfed her as she wondered what had happened to the bodies in the clearing during the night. What ought she to do? The last thing she wanted was to go up again to the scene of devastation, but all her identity seemed to lie there in those dead bodies. She shuddered, buried her face in her hands, and twisted from side to side. Gradually her anguish eased. She seated herself very quietly on a rock and watched the rising mist.

A rustle in the grass drew her attention to a fallen

tree trunk, silver-gray with age and well mossed. A tiny head peeked out of a knothole and looked about. Its nose wiggled busily. Out popped the chipmunk, followed almost immediately by another. The two carried on busy communication, chitting and chatting as they darted about, gathering food. Their red-brown coats blended with the leaf-strewn forest floor and at those moments when they paused it was difficult for her to spot them.

So too was another visitor difficult to spot, his rusty brown coat blending so well into the landscape that the busy chipmunks did not notice him. The fox's eyes were wary and alert as he looked from her to the chipmunks. Faith opened her mouth to give warning but was too late. In a sudden spring the fox caught one of the little creatures by the neck. The chipmunk gave but one squeak before the fox's jaws clamped down. It hung limply. The fox melted away.

For a time both Faith and the other chipmunk remained immobile. Then the little creature began to wander aimlessly back and forth. He seemed bereft without his fellow. After awhile he stopped and sat on the fallen tree trunk. His head jerked from side to side as he peered about. His steady chittering was so soft it could scarcely be heard.

The sun rose a little higher and a faint breeze rustled the leaves along the ravine. Before long the chipmunk was hunting food again. He was a little subdued, but even that did not last for long. Gradually he became almost as lively as he had been before the tragic event.

As Faith watched the chipmunk, she felt a sense of kinship with it. This is the way it goes, she thought. Life cannot go on if too much attention is paid to death. The important thing is to get on with the living. After all, what choice did the little chipmunk have?

What choice did she have?

Faith went back to the cave. With great care she stepped around the motionless dog and took down the cheese. After the first bite her throat closed and it was impossible to swallow. She could almost feel Papa's frowning gaze. "Eat, child, you must keep up your strength." That from Papa, who, when he got discussing theology, often forgot all about the food on his plate.

There must be a swarm of jays and ravens in the settlement clearing. They were cawing and screaming and, after the quiet of the morning, sounded particularly noisy. Someone or something, Faith realized, must have come to upset the birds so. Indians? Fear clamped down on her with a band of ice. If Indians had come they would surely find Blanche. Then Blanche would, sooner or later, lead them to the cave.

Faith could hear Blanche noisily eating below. The goat yanked at branches until they snapped. As she scrambled over the rocks her hooves clicked and rattled the smaller stones. Faith would have called to Blanche but she was afraid that she would find herself unable, as before, to speak the words. If the goat stayed there, making noise, it would make sense for Faith to hurry away as rapidly as possible. But if she left she would have to leave Moses behind. She would never leave Moses!

She crouched close to the dog. He lay in the same position as before, his body cold and stiff. He couldn't be dead, not Moses! Panic, like cold metal, gripped her.

Blinding light filled the cave. Faith gasped at the silhouette of a man. After a long moment the man spoke, surprise making his voice loud: "Miss Faith! You are safe!"

She recognized the voice. It was Sergeant Stedman. Now she also recognized the sturdy frame of the guide. He knelt down next to her. Now that the sunlight shone on him from the side, and her eyes were better accustomed to it, she could see his face. It looked different from the way she remembered it. Before it had been so stern — now there was kindness there and an almost frightened look.

"Miss Faith, are you all right?"

She shrank back, unable to speak. She looked at Moses.

The sergeant leaned forward and touched the dog. "He's dead?"

Faith felt as if she would cry, but then the feeling left. A coldness inside of her had hardened it up.

"When did he die?"

She hung her head. He touched her arm gently, then she lifted her head, her eyes blank.

"Faith, talk to me."

She squeezed her eyes shut so tightly that they hurt.

She forgot what he had asked. She felt the pressure of the man's hand on her shoulder. "Faith, come with me."

She allowed herself to be led from the cave. The guide crossed his arms and studied her.

"Faith, have you been up at the settlement since the massacre?"

She thought about this. The words seemed to come from far away. They echoed in her head before she understood them. Slowly she nodded.

He gave a deep sigh, then said, "There are two men who came here with me. They are up in the settlement. It would help us a great deal if you could identify some of the bodies we have found. Would you be willing to do that for us?"

Again she nodded.

"Good. I want you to go up there with me. But wait. Have you eaten recently?"

It seemed too difficult a question to answer. She turned and started up the path. She could hear his footsteps behind her. They made a good sound.

Their appearance at the top of the ravine startled the two men in the clearing. The men called and waved. Faith shrank back against the sergeant and grabbed his arm. He guided her up to them.

His voice was reassuring. "These are friends: Captain Mason and Mr. Haynes." He held up a hand to quell their questions. "Mistress Faith Ralston is new to the colony. She is still upset by her experiences. I found her in a cave by the spring."

Faith saw that these two men were very different from the sergeant. Stedman's skin was burned dark, his body was muscular, and his clothing was dull and practical. His face was close to expressionless most of the time, except for the dark gray eyes, and his features looked as if hewn from wood. One of the men was tall, spare, and pale. He peered at her with obvious curiosity. The other one was florid, well along in age, and had a great sagging belly that made it look as if he never labored. Both were better mannered than the guide, however, for they bobbed their heads properly, just as if there were not dead bodies lying around the clearing. Faith turned away.

From the corner of her eyes she could see that they did not know what to make of her. The tall man simply raised his eyebrows when he looked toward the sergeant, but the other tapped his own skull with a forefinger. So, he thought she was crazy. She wondered if she were.

Sergeant Stedman ignored the men's suggestive grimaces and let his eyes scan the devastated area. "We have found five bodies. We have been able to identify Master Keene, your father, and Master Sedgewick. We found Ralph's body by the stream. That leaves only one body to identify, but we are missing Goodman Young and young Peter Eaton as well as Goodman Brown. Can you identify the body for us?"

When she did not respond he went on. "Miss Faith, we have to know. We can be fairly certain that the Indians took the women and girls. That is their custom.

Evidently they also took the young lads and perhaps one of the men. If we don't know which ones, we can't negotiate for their return.''

At this Faith looked at him.

''If captives live to reach the territory up north where there are some French, and if we have their names and descriptions, we can sometimes succeed in ransoming them. We go to Boston and an emissary from Boston goes to Canada. In this way the colonists have dealt with the French in many cases. A captive may be sent home if an emissary goes with the proper description and ransom.''

How would little Betty manage to walk to Canada? Poor Mistress Keene could scarcely manage to walk around her house, and old Mistress Sedgewick — at the thought of her Faith had to bite down panic.

Only then did Faith remember that she had not seen Peter's body. She walked to the row of bodies the men had laid out. It was Goodman Young whom they could not name. She knew him by the unburned remnants of his clothing. There was one other adult male for them to find. She led them to where Goodman Brown lay, mostly hidden under rubble. As well as Peter, the Brown boys and the Keene twins were missing. She opened her mouth to speak, but nothing came out.

She wanted to talk. If Peter and the boys were alive she wanted them to be ransomed. She longed to see Peter's familiar face. She stared at the sergeant, shaking with the attempt to speak.

Finally Sergeant Stedman produced a piece of birch

bark and a sharp stick. She laboriously wrote the names of the two bodies and lay the labels down upon them.

"Now write down the names of as many of the missing as you remember." Sergeant Stedman handed her another sheet of bark.

Faith sat down on the charred doorstep of the remains of the Keene house and wrote the list. As she wrote she began to feel better. There were many missing. All the women and children except for herself. Maybe they would be ransomed and she would see them again. The weird feeling was beginning to pass. She began to feel some sadness and less fear. Her eyes sought out the sergeant. He and the other two men were digging graves, working steadily. She felt safe with the sergeant there.

11 ❧ *Sergeant Stedman*

❧ "See here, Sergeant," said the red-faced man, passing his arm over his sweating forehead. "I've a real anxiety about getting on to Brookfield. There are a lot of folks I know up there. I'd feel mighty relieved if I could know this hasn't happened there."

The thinner man nodded. "Was thinking that myself. Ground digs easy here. Can you handle this by yourself, Sergeant?" His grizzled face showed concern as he pointed his chin at Faith. "You are the one to handle this situation methinks, seeing as the girl is in the shape she is and you having known her before."

"Aye." Stedman frowned. Even Faith could tell that he would rather they stayed. Of course, under the circumstances they were eager to go on. Faith could not bring herself to make eye contact with either of them; she kept her eyes on the sergeant almost constantly.

"Aye," he repeated. "I'll bury the dead and get the girl to Springfield."

Captain Mason cleared his throat. "Women might be able to do something for her." His gaze slid over to Faith and away again rapidly. "We'll be expecting to see you in Marlborough by Wednesday next."

Stedman nodded. "I'll be there."

The other two men nodded at each other. Relief softened the tautness of their bodies. Mr. Haynes's expression as he looked at Faith became one of kindliness. "Eh, miss, you'll be feeling better soon. A young girl who has been through all this — it's bound to hit hard."

He stepped closer and patted her shoulder awkwardly. "Time is a greater healer, my dear. As the Good Book says, 'The Lord giveth and the Lord taketh away.' It's beyond our understanding why these things happen. Just trust in the Lord."

Faith swallowed. A fly buzzed loudly around her ear.

"Come on," said Captain Mason in a loud whisper. "She ain't even hearing you, Haynes." Then in a louder whisper: "I've seen 'em like this before, Sergeant. Shock, of course. Some folks pull out real good. Don't rush her though."

They nodded good-bye, slung their muskets over their shoulders, and were gone.

It seemed to Faith that with their departure the sun became warmer. For a few minutes she stood and watched the sergeant while he shoveled. The sunlight was bright, but the shadows of a beech tree played over him. For a moment she thought she was looking at Peter. Then she realized it could not be Peter because Peter was taller and thinner. Then she thought it might be Papa, but then Papa had not possessed the strength to lift a shovelful of dirt with such grace. Of course, Ralph . . . for a moment it was Ralph she saw until the memory of how he had looked lying at the edge of the stream cut across her thoughts like a knife.

"You saw Ralph at the stream?" she asked clearly.

He looked up, startled. He paused, resting on his shovel, before he answered.

"We brought him up here and laid him with the others. It seems to me that he would like being buried with them. Also, it's easier." He gestured to the row of bodies. The heads were all covered.

The sergeant wiped the sweat off his brow. "There is another shovel if you want to use it, Miss Faith."

She went over and picked it up. It was so heavy she had difficulty carrying it the few feet to the digging spot. She pushed the shovel down with strong pressure from her booted foot. She tilted it back until it broke the earth. Her body strained to lift it, her thin wrists quivering with the effort.

Stedman stepped over and pulled the shovel away. "That was a mistake. I did not realize you were so thin."

The unfocused look was returning to her eyes.

"I do need some other help you can give. Find a Bible and search out a passage that is good for burials."

She nodded and moved off, her thin shoulders drooping. She found Papa's Bible among the supplies they had carried from the cave.

The gravesite was now ready for the bodies to be dragged into it.

When he saw her looking blankly at the Bible he said, "I want you to read from Psalms. When you finish reading Psalms, go on to the Gospel according to Luke."

Her fingers were rough on the delicate pages. She found Psalms. Instead of reading she watched as he bent over to pick up the first body.

He stood, holding it, and they stared at each other. The smell of the overturned earth, the fire, and the bodies rose in the afternoon heat. The air between them wavered. It was difficult to see him.

"Faith," he said loudly. "You must stand under the pine so there is shade on the pages. Face downhill. Your voice should carry on the wind."

His voice was strong and firm and the hazy air disappeared. She nodded and walked over to the pine. She would read the Bible for Papa while he was laid to rest. While he had lived she had done little for Papa without resentment. Now there was little she could do for him at all. She wished he knew she was going to read for him.

" 'Blessed is the man that walketh not in the counsel of the ungodly, nor standest in the way of the sinners, nor sitteth in the seat of the scornful. But his delight is in the law of the Lord; and in his law doth he meditate day and night.' "

Her clear voice went on. Out of the corner of her eyes she saw the bodies laid down, one after another. She turned when she saw the big dog being added to the row. She heard the thud of dirt as it hit the bodies but her voice did not falter.

Finally the beauty of the words and the rhythm of the reading brought her a measure of peace. From time to time she looked at the sergeant and she could see that the words were working on him also. Psalm 20 pleased her so much that she read it five times in succession.

Twice she stopped her reading when the sergeant, pausing for a swallow of water, passed the jug to her. By the time she was worn from reading, the burials were completed.

"Thank you, Faith," said the sergeant. "You are a fine reader of scripture."

"What do we do now?"

"Now we will eat. There will be only a short time for eating before the day is done. Tonight we will sleep in the cave. Tomorrow we will walk to Springfield."

"With Blanche," she said firmly.

"With Blanche."

He made a small fire away from the charred buildings but within the clearing, just below the root cellar where there was a dip in the land. She knew by now that he had chosen the site so that the flame would not show at a distance. With the stench that still hung over the clearing, it would take a very sharp nose to identify the smell of this fire. The sergeant put a pot with grain and water over the coals. While the porridge cooked, he searched through the dimming light for objects to save.

"I am putting all things worth saving into the cellar hole," he told her. "We will hide the opening before we leave. Someday one of us will return and retrieve those items we can use.''

After this, neither one made conversation. Day quickly became night. Evening wind came from the north, blessedly clear and fresh, but cold enough to turn the fingers blue. The sergeant's activities became more hurried. He went for two blankets he had retrieved. Without setting them down he stomped out the fire.

"Come," he said.

He led the way down to the spring and up the path she and Blanche had broken to the cave. Blanche, like a vague white ghost, could be seen above them. The sergeant reached down and pulled Faith up, his hand strong. The goat nudged them happily.

"Stay here," ordered the sergeant and left, to return minutes later with a pile of leaves.

The sergeant prepared the cave for sleeping by piling leaves on the floor. The goat knew what was expected of her and lay down contentedly and started eating her bed. Faith laid herself down painfully. The long days of tension had left her muscles stiff and sore. The sergeant spread a blanket over her and then lay down beside her. He turned his back to her and faced the opening of the cave. He arranged the musket beside him and held a knife in his hand. He pulled back the stick that had propped up the dry grass overhang and the cave became dark.

The goat made a sound between a sigh and a snort and settled down to sleep. Faith, now safe and cared for, relaxed. She felt as if she were floating and drifting down, down into a black void. She was all enclosed. Where she lay, the roof of the cave was only two feet above her nose. There was cave wall and goat tight up on one side and the backside of a man tight up against the other side.

"I'm in a grave," she said in a hushed tone. "I'm not going to wake up alive."

"Nonsense," said Sergeant Stedman. "Go to sleep."

The leaves were comfortable. She was warm. This night the dreams were not so bad.

12 ❧ *Springfield*

❧ Sergeant Stedman stopped at the brow of the hill and pointed. "Springfield."

Faith roused herself from her well of misery and lifted her head. They had started out in the gray of early morning and had been walking almost continuously. Images from the past few days filled her mind and she had noticed little along the way. Now she obediently looked in the direction of his pointing finger. There was a house in the distance ahead on a hill.

"Ralph said Springfield was on a river."

"The Connecticut. That's out of sight beyond the hills."

They resumed walking. A few more houses appeared, looking peaceful under the afternoon sun. "I thought you said the town had been burned early this fall, before you met us in Boston."

"The Indians burned it October fifth. The part of town

on the west side of the river suffered most from the burning. Here quite a few houses were spared, especially the outlying ones. Mine escaped the fire and is unharmed — at least it was the last time I saw it — and it is one of the buildings farthest from the center.''

She looked at him curiously. Usually when he spoke he was matter-of-fact, but this time there was emotion in his voice. From the way he spoke, she could imagine the fire with the acrid smell of burning. She could see Indians and flames, and people running out into the cold.

''After their houses burned, where did people live?''

''Wherever they could find a roof to cover their heads. There were about fifteen houses in the town center that were saved and almost everyone wanted to move into one of those. No one likes living in a garrison any longer than is absolutely necessary. There is even less privacy there than on board ship. When I left, the garrison remained crowded and the houses in town were jammed, yet few were willing to risk going into the more outlying homes.''

''Where will I live?'' Steeped in misery as she was, she had not thought of the future.

''That depends on the Reverend Mr. Glover. He makes most of the decisions now. But Mr. Glover may be too busy to tend to your needs. People from all over come to him with their problems and he has some of his own — he lost all his possessions when his house was burned. If he is too busy to deal with your problems, probably Goody Collins will decide what to do for you. She has been as a mother to me for years. I'm taking you to her.''

Faith said nothing. She felt strangely numb, as if she were not really present but instead nearby, watching herself. It seemed as if all the events of the past few days had happened to someone else. Memories slipped in and out of her mind like bits of bad dreams.

She had tried to tell the sergeant how she felt. "Don't worry," he had said. "Given time you will feel normal again."

When she did remember, she discovered that she was recalling things she would never have expected to. She was surprised to find that she missed the Keenes, every last obnoxious one of them. She missed Peter also, almost as much as she missed Papa.

Blanche nudged her, nibbling at the braid that hung over her shoulder. Faith lay a hand against the goat's warm neck.

As they labored up the side of the last hill, Faith felt incredibly weary. She blinked hard to keep her eyes open and stiffened her neck. The walk to Springfield had not been so many miles, but the sergeant seemed to have forgotten how tired she was and had set a rapid pace. Her clothing was now so soiled that it chafed her skin. There had been no way to get the streaks of blood and soot out of it. She knew she smelled — she could smell herself as she moved. They had not eaten since breakfast, and she was hungry.

The sergeant stopped short and she almost bumped into him. She looked across the valley and now she could see more of the town. There was a square with a few houses around it, a meetinghouse, and beyond, a garrison. Further along, almost out of sight, was another garrison.

"There on the side of North Hill stands my house."

There was almost a smile on his face and a touch of pride to his tone. It was one of the few times he had allowed himself much emotion. She looked and saw only a forested hillside with a spot where there might be a clearing. "Oh," she said doubtfully.

"You'll see it later. First we will go to see Goody Collins."

The house to which he now pointed looked substantial and attractive. The diamond-paned windows reflected the afternoon sun. It reminded her of a house in Sussex.

"Why is it standing when all the others near it were burned?" Faith looked at it accusingly as if she thought the owners had made a pact with the Indians.

"Who knows?" Stedman glanced at her and saw that she was disturbed. "Who knows why God plans for things to happen as they do?"

She grabbed his arm. "Do you truly think that it was God who planned for me to live and others to die?" She gave her head a hard shake. "It should not be, you know, if God is fair. Papa was a much more Godfearing person than I have ever been. It isn't fair that he, who was pious, should die and I, so unworthy, should live."

The sergeant's thick brows drew together in a frown. "That's not how things go," he said impatiently. "You know — fairly. Life often isn't fair. You can't possibly understand why things like that happen. You just have to accept what happens and cope with it.''

She shoved the knuckle of her fisted right hand into her mouth and bit down until the pain ran up her arm.

''I feel so guilty about being alive,'' she whispered.

''Life is a gift. It is not earned. It is not a reward for good behavior. You are not given the choice of whether or not you will be alive; you can only choose how you will attend to the life you have.''

She swallowed hard and tried to listen to what he was saying. The ideas slid away, slippery as fish.

Faith tugged at the goat's lead and Blanche started moving again.

They walked the rest of the way in silence. As they came closer to the house Faith saw the blackened remains of other buildings up and down the street.

''She may not be here,'' warned the sergeant. ''When a warning has been put out, everyone in town goes to a garrison until it has been deemed safe to return home. Goody hates the garrison so she'll be here if she possibly can.''

''She's inside,'' said Faith, seeing through the window that someone was moving inside.

The door suddenly opened. The woman who stood there reminded Faith of nothing so much as the round apple dumplings that Auntie Abbie used to make for her. Her round-cheeked face was framed by a crisp white cap and her short, wide body was dressed in yards of a brown-sprigged print.

"Zachary!" Her happy tone was a warm welcome. "I didn't know we'd be seeing you so soon."

"We found disaster in High Hills," he said as he entered.

They stood and looked at each other quietly, the woman, the man, and the girl. Dust motes caught the afternoon sun. The bright fire sparked. Faith became more aware of how cold she had been these last days.

"There was a raid there, a massacre. We found only Faith alive."

Faith did not want to look at the woman's face as she listened. "Blanche needs attention," she mumbled, backing out of the house. She retained a confused impression of tidiness and warmth, but she felt more at ease outside. The sergeant followed her out, reached for the rope dangling from Blanche's neck, and guided the goat to an enclosure in back.

"Come in, child." Goody Collins stood in the doorway. She was assessing Faith, but her expression was kind. "Come have some ale and bread. We will see what we can do to make you comfortable."

The door shut, enclosing them in comfort and warmth.

"It's getting on winter, isn't it?" said Faith.

She stood uneasily near the hearth as Goody bobbed this way and that, adjusting the kettle over the fire, peeking into the oven, taking mugs from the shelf — all the while darting quick glances that seemed to see Faith inside and out.

"November the fifth it is today," said Goody. "I keep good track of the calendar, but it is easy to tell that winter is coming. More geese flying south there are, all the time. Must be all on their way by now. Frost on the glazing until well into the morning. Be no time until it snows.''

Faith nodded. Her throat had knotted and she knew that words would not come out.

Goody shot a sharp look at her and clucked. ''Best sit, child . . . there, by the fire. I'll get you some hot tisane too.''

Faith sat and smelled the fragrance of the brewing herbal tea as it spread through the air. The sergeant came back in, letting a blast of cold air in with him. He spoke and Faith liked the tone of his voice. It was deep and even and it made her feel calm and safe. ''Can you keep Faith here, Goody? How many folks do you have billeted on you?''

''When I get them, five. But they are all soldiers. Men without families. No one else wanted them because of all the cooking and their not being around to help much. But me, I like to cook. Still, they are gone most of the time.'' She smiled on Faith and nodded. ''I'd be mighty pleased to care for Faith, Zachary. This is probably the best place for her.''

''Good. I'm eager to get over to my own house now. No one has moved into it since I left, have they?''

''Lands, no.'' Goody chuckled comfortably. ''No one wants to be over there. Too far from the center of things.''

The sergeant sat on the stool next to the table and drank the steaming ale that Goody poured for him. Every time Faith looked up he was watching her but then his eyes slid away. The silence became awkward. After what seemed like a long time he set his mug down and stood.

"Get some rest now, Miss Faith. You can trust Goody as if . . . as if she were that aunt of yours. I'll take Blanche with me."

Faith nodded. She still could not trust herself to speak. She clutched the edge of her seat as the sergeant left. Through the window she could see him return to the enclosure. He and Blanche walked up the street and out of her sight. Faith felt weak and was trembling.

"There, there, now," said Goody comfortingly. "Maybe a bit of a wash and some sleep, eh? You look as if you could use some sleep. My daughter had a bedgown that will do for you. Come along, my dear."

13 ❧ Goodwife Collins

❧ A shaft of sunlight tickled her eyelids. Faith twisted her head and tried to burrow deeper into the covers. Twisting pulled the coverlet off her feet. Cold rushed up to replace the warmth. Faith squeezed her eyes tightly shut. She did not want to awaken.

Despite her efforts to ward it off, memory flooded in and the last vestiges of sleep vanished. Faith sat up. She had been well wrapped in bed. She lay atop one feather mattress and another covered her. Her clothing clung to her and the hair at the back of her neck was wet.

Across the room Goody was bent over the hearth, the flames of the fire flickering across her broad cheeks. Yesterday Faith had not noticed how similar Goodwife Collins was to Auntie Abbie's housekeeper. And that white cap—imagine a white cap when whole settlements were burning!

Goody looked up and smiled her good morning, her cheeks getting even rounder. "Porridge is here should you want it."

The porridge was warm and perfectly cooked. Faith savored every bite. When Goody bent to tend the fire Faith quickly picked up the trencher and licked it out.

It felt as if the food were bringing new energy into her. "Almost," she thought, "as if I were a corpse come to life." The thought brought back horrendous images and she shuddered. Suddenly she couldn't wait to get clean.

"Is there a comb I might use?" she asked. "It would please me greatly to wash and comb."

The wash water was so cold Faith's fingers turned blue before she was through. It occurred to her that winter was almost upon them and that she had no clothing but the borrowed nightdress she wore now and the clothing she had worn yesterday. The loss of her clothing touched off a feeling of being painfully alone and she felt sorry for herself. As she combed her hair she yanked and pulled at the knots in the long strands. Tears came to her eyes. Sunk in gloom, she hoped Goody would notice and think her tears to be tears of pain.

Her hair soon hung in its long tidy plait. Goody appeared with a simple gray gown that looked warm and serviceable and blessedly clean. "My Suzanna had this gown," explained Goody. "I'd be happy to have you use it. Died five years ago, she did. No point hanging onto it anymore. Not with such need around."

Faith began to stammer her thanks.

"Shush, shush," said Goody. "Here, let me help you with the buttons."

Such a pleasure it was to wear a clean gown. Such a

pleasure to look down at her skirt and not see streaks
of blood, blood that reminded her of terror and fear and
loss and loneliness.

"Now we'll go to Zachary's house," said Goody.

Along their way a tall gentleman approached them
purposefully. The dour lines of his craggy face were
emphasized by dark, heavy eyebrows. Thin to the point
of emaciation, he looked like a skeleton with his clothes
hanging from his broad shoulders.

"Goody Collins," he trumpeted loudly.

Goody stopped so abruptly that Faith knocked into
her. "Mr. Glover."

Mr. Glover took Faith's hands in his own. "You poor
dear lamb," he intoned so loudly that Faith thought the
whole town must hear. "My heart goes out to you. Such
trials, such tribulations! The Lord is trying you, my
child, trying you."

Faith bit her tongue and stared at the ground.

"Mute — and no wonder. How you suffer, how we
all suffer from these grievous losses!" He shook his
hands up and down to emphasize his point. Since Faith's
hands were imprisoned in his, they too went up and
down. A pleased note came into his voice when he spoke
next. "We have plans for you, never doubt it."

Faith looked up in alarm. He and Goody were nodding
at each other, apparently pleased with something they
had planned. An uneasiness penetrated her gloom.

She was relieved when he left them. He walked away,
his back straight and stiff with determination, as if he
knew just what ought to be done and was determined

to see it done. Faith wondered if he was correct in what he had said; had God planned the massacre to try her? The idea frightened her.

Goody Collins headed toward a house set much apart from the others, uphill away from the town. The front door of the house faced downhill. When they reached it Faith looked back and could see the river, a trail below, and hills off in the distance.

"I like this house," she said.

Goody beamed with pride. "About six years ago, Zachary and my son Ranulf put up this house," she said. "Young as they were, they were two of the most skilled men in this whole town. It's made as fine as you'll find. Wouldn't let another soul touch it, that proud they were."

"Your son lives here, too?"

"No, no. He helped because Suzanna was going to marry Zachary. My Suzanna and Ranulf were twins. Dead five years now, both of them. Fever, it was."

Sergeant Stedman's house was fronted on one side with a high fence over which a sheep and chickens could be seen. As the women stepped to the door the fence shook slightly as another creature got up to peer at them. Large yellow eyes appeared at the railing.

"Blanche!" Faith stepped close and scratched Blanche around her wattles.

The large yellow eyes blinked and the goat thrust out her chin for more. Blanche was her old friend. There was no other creature she knew of alive who knew what the massacre had been like. Looking at Blanche reminded her of the smell of the fire and the sight of the bodies swarming with flies.

She lost what fragile control she had. She did not even notice Goody Collins watching as the tears ran down her cheeks.

Goody grabbed her elbow and guided her into the house. "Zachary?" she called. "I've brought the orphan." Then, in a loud whisper, "She's that upset. Best sit her down."

She was vaguely aware that the sergeant was beside her, pushing her down into a chair near the hearth. She grabbed his hand. "Poor Papa, poor Papa . . ." She could see Papa as clearly as if he stood before her: the worn leathern breeches, the old, gray-brown coat rubbed shiny at the elbows, the bald head that reflected the firelight. How unsuited he had been to life in these rugged colonies, how childlike in his earnest piety. Now that she was no longer trapped by his blind devotion to his principles they began to appear as high ideals.

Poor, pompous, foolish Master Keene. Whatever his faults, he was an idealistic man who struggled daily to understand the words of the Bible. How startled he must have been to see the Indians. And kindly Master Sedgewick — how friendly he had been to her. None of them deserved to die. It was so unfair!

And poor Mistress Keene and Goodwife Young and the other women — it must be so terrifying to be with the Indians. She knew they would suffer not only for themselves but would also suffer the anguish of being unable to help the children.

"There, there," said Goody over and over, patting Faith on the shoulder. "Just what she needs," she said to the sergeant.

"Do you think so?" he asked doubtfully. He took a large handkerchief and wiped Faith's eyes awkwardly. "Seems to me she's worn out enough without crying so."

Faith paid no heed but wept until exhaustion overcame her. Finally she sniffed, wiped a shaking arm across her eyes, and was quiet. The frenzy of weeping had led to a deadened resignation. She felt tired now and cold. She shivered.

The sergeant threw wood on the fire until it crackled and its flames lit up the room. When that did not stop her shivering he brought a blanket woven of rough wool which he and Goody wrapped about her.

She took one last shuddering breath and then sat silently, staring at the fire. She hoped that Papa had been dead before the house burned. If he had just lain there helpless, fearing the burning . . . she shook her head to dispel the images.

"Mistress Faith. *Faith*!" The sergeant spoke very loudly, as if she were deaf. He gripped her wrist and shook it.

She looked at him, seeing him as if for the first time. How strong he looked with his broad shoulders blocking out the light from the window. An Indian would probably be afraid to come at him, even with a knife in hand. His chin was so firm. He looked determined and powerful — there wasn't that faintly childish cast that had lain over Papa's face, nor the weak, petulant expression that had sometimes settled on Master Keene's, nor the weary resignation and helplessness that had characterized Mistress Keene.

She grabbed his hand. "Do you think that God had them killed to try me?" she asked.

The sergeant stared at Goody Collins.

"That's what Mr. Glover told her on the way over here," she explained.

"I wouldn't want to disagree with the minister," he said carefully, "but I don't think he means you personally. I think he means that all the sinning of the people here in the colonies is causing God to punish them."

"But Papa didn't sin!" she wailed.

"I know, I know," he said hastily. "You see, it is all so awful that people want to know why it is happening. No one likes to think that things happen without reason. The clergymen don't really know the answers either."

"The Reverend Mr. Glover is a very learned man, Zachary," pointed out Goody uneasily.

"Certainly he is, but that does not mean that God has revealed all the answers to him."

"What do you think?" Faith asked.

"I think about it a lot, but I don't know why people are suffering so. I do think it is logical for the Indians to fight the English. There are some English people who are pointlessly cruel to the Indians. It is such a problem, for we want this land and the Indians want it too. We are very different people. I don't know if it will ever be possible for us to live in peace together."

Goody stirred uneasily beside Faith. "Surely, Zachary, given time . . ."

His voice was hard and clipped. "Given time things will only get worse."

Faith hiccupped. "My Auntie Abbie says that God is love. If that is so, why does He allow such terrible things to happen?"

"God is also a jealous God," stated Goody.

"I believe God is love, also," said the sergeant. "But God is many other things, too. I think it is more than we can understand. It is, anyway, more than I can understand. I think it is important, Faith, for all people to do their best in every situation until we know more."

Faith's face lightened. "That sounds almost like something my Auntie Abbie would say. I also remember she used to tell me that a person should never borrow trouble, that most people have enough of their own."

"Very good advice," said Goody, sounding easier. "You certainly have enough trouble without wondering if it was somehow your fault."

For a while there was silence; then Goody finally spoke. "You especially asked Faith to come over here, Zachary."

"I wanted to ask her to take care of the goat and the other animals while I am gone this time."

Faith felt fear, cold and tight. "Why do you have to go?"

"There may be other settlements that have suffered

as did High Hills. There may be others awaiting help as you were.''

"Oh.''

''The lad who usually cares for my animals when I'm away has joined the militia. Will you take care of them this time?''

At this Faith nodded. She would rather he stayed, but the house and the animals felt like a part of him. She liked the idea that until the sergeant returned they would be her responsibility. It would feel like being near him.

''Are you going to be fearful coming here since my house is out of the center of things?''

She shook her head. She didn't want him to get some-one else for the job.

His face showed concern. ''A lot of people are afraid to come here and you, with what you have been through . . .''

She knew she would not be afraid. ''You see, it's your place,'' she said. ''I feel safer around you than anyone else. I like being in your house.''

''Now, Zachary,'' said Goody, ''I think that gives you a definite answer. Your animals will be in good hands.''

❧   The aroma of bread wafted out to the garden behind Goody's house where Goody and Faith were piling leaves around the rosebush. One of the few rosebushes in Springfield, it had, according to Goody, survived five winters since its arrival.

"And it's going to get through this winter, too, even if the people don't," said Goody with grim determination, huffing as she knelt to cover the plant for the winter.

Dirt streaks showed on Goody's cheeks as she raised her head to study the sky. "Any moment now, I'll warrant," she predicted, referring to the snow they were preparing against. "Less'n it's a bad blow and rain. Freezing rain it'd be." She blew on her frigid fingers. "You go in and get that bread out of the oven, Faith. I'm not going to stand until this is done."

The warmth of the hot bricks felt good to hands prickling with cold. Using the greatest care, Faith slid the oven shovel in and took out the eight loaves she had formed. One for every day of the week plus another loaf to give away.

Faith set the loaves in a row on the table to cool: round, brown, and hot. She had made the bread and was proud. Auntie Abbie had insisted that she learn to bake bread and she had always received much praise for her skill.

By the time she had cleaned out the oven and tamped down the coals Goody was back inside.

"Did you know that Zachary returned last night? Well, he said he'd be gone a week, didn't he? Reliable as they come, is Zachary. Dropped by late. You were asleep." She warmed her hands at the oven. "I want you to take over the extra loaf to him. Wrap it in the linen hanging nigh the fire."

Faith was happy that the sergeant had returned. It had been a difficult week. She liked being with Goody because she was so easy to talk with. She had told Goody all the horrors of the massacre, over and over. She also liked being at the sergeant's house, where the animals greeted her enthusiastically and where she knew she was useful. What she had not liked were the curious townspeople she met as she walked from one house to the other. Today Faith had gone only half the distance to the sergeant's house before she was accosted by two little boys, thin and freckled children, who bombarded her with questions.

"Tell us about the massacre, Mistress. What did you see? How did they sound? How did you know to hide ahead of time? How does an Indian go about scalping? Did you have an ax, Mistress?''

Faith twisted uncomfortably. She did not know how to answer them. She would not talk with them. She had to steel herself to keep from dashing away.

''Ah, Miss Faith.''

The voice of authority quieted the boys immediately. Faith had not thought she would ever welcome the overbearing clergyman.

''My dear young lady,'' the clergyman began, and cleared his throat. ''You are well met. I was on my way to speak with you. I have discussed your situation with Goodwife Collins and Sergeant Stedman and we have all come to the same conclusion: that is, that it would be best for you to be married and we think you should marry the sergeant.''

''Married!''

''It is the best arrangement if the proper man is available and it seems that we could not do better than to marry you to Sergeant Stedman.''

''Marry the sergeant?''

''Sergeant Stedman is the only man at all suitable and he is willing to serve you in this way.''

''Oh, no. Oh, no, no, sir.''

''You dislike the sergeant so much?''

''Oh, no. But I'm sure he is just offering because he thinks he has to.''

''Of course. Sergeant Stedman knows his duty.''

''I know. Yes, he does. But, sir, I cannot marry him.''

The clergyman looked at her askance, his heavy dark

brows raised. "Young lady, as I understand it you have no home, no family, and no money. We are in the middle of a war. We have a shortage of houses, there has been death in almost every family, there is a shortage of food, and it is going to get worse. Winter is upon us. What do you propose to do?"

Faith opened her mouth and shut it again. The sergeant doesn't want me, she wanted to yell at him, but somehow, the way the clergyman spoke, that didn't seem very important.

"The sergeant is needed by the militia and will be away for some time. You can care for his home and animals. You will have food to eat and a roof over your head. It is not reasonable to expect Goody Collins to care for you indefinitely, you know."

"Yes, I know." Faith hung her head and clutched the bread tightly to her. Without looking up, she managed to curtsy, then hurried up the hill, scuttling along like some small wild animal.

Halfway up the hill the tumult inside her head had begun to calm and anger began to take over. Why did other people always run her life? For years it was Auntie Abbie who always told her what to do. Then Auntie Abbie handed her over to Papa and Papa had practically handed her over to the Keenes. Now Goody and Mr. Glover wanted to decide her life. Was she ever going to be able to make choices for herself?

By the time she reached Sergeant Stedman's house she was shaking. If he became her husband he would have the right to determine the rest of her life. As she considered this, she became calmer. One thing she knew definitely about the sergeant — he would be fair to her if they were married. If she had to marry she could not find anyone with a stricter sense of fairness. In addition, he was unlikely to beat her as some men beat their wives, and she didn't think he would take her for granted the way Master Keene had done with Mistress Keene.

She set her jaw firmly. She had come across the ocean on that awful boat, she had learned to get along with Papa and the Keenes, and she had survived a massacre. Surely marriage could not be much worse.

As she stepped onto the path to the door, she heard a noise in the yard at the far side of the house. Faith walked quietly to the corner and peeked around. The sergeant was trying to grab a lively puppy that was dashing back and forth just out of reach. Its long brown ears flapped and its pink tongue hung out. The sergeant gave a disgusted snort and sat back on his heels. The puppy plopped down too, still out of reach. It cocked its head to one side and looked at the sergeant. Faith could have sworn it was laughing.

She giggled.

Zachary Stedman was on his feet in a flash. The puppy raced to her and jumped up. She scratched it behind the ears and giggled again. The giggle surprised her. She had thought she would never be able to laugh again.

"Hold him," said the sergeant. He came up with a rope collar and slipped it over the puppy's head. "There now. I've wasted the better part of the last half-hour trying to grab this fellow."

Faith handed him the bread and sank to her knees. The puppy kissed her enthusiastically. She hugged it and laughed. As she laughed, she discovered that she was also crying. She blinked away the tears.

"Where did he come from?"

"From the Northfield area. We came across a deserted farm. Indians had not gotten at it but the owners had evidently taken off for fear that they would. Must have taken all the other animals with them. We found just this fellow hiding out behind the house. Looks like a hound-type dog. I thought he'd make you a good pet."

"Me?" She gave a short laugh. "Me? How will I feed him?"

The sergeant turned brick red.

"I thought that Goody would have told you."

"Told me what?" she cried, her voice shrill.

His expression became more wooden than ever. She glared at him but he would not meet her eyes. Her throat constricted.

"Is it all set?" she whispered.

"Yes. This afternoon Mr. Glover will meet us at Goody's house." He cleared his throat with difficulty. "It's the best thing for us, you know," he said loudly. "I didn't like the idea at first because — well, I'm not likely to survive the war, the way things are going — and I didn't think it was fair to put you through any more losses. But then, you aren't attached to me so perhaps that's not so bad. And there is no one else to take you in. Even Goody is overburdened.

"And for me, too, it is good. I have no one else to

leave my house to. Of course, a lot of folks might want it, but I've no relations. At least you'll have a roof over your head if I get killed.''

He was right, of course.

He had to lean forward to hear her whispered, ''Why so soon?''

''I have to leave again tomorrow. This will give me one night to show you around some more. You'll need more instructions about the way things are done in the house and the barn. I'll be away a lot longer this time than I was last time.''

The puppy pushed against her legs, annoyed at being ignored. She patted it absently.

''One night? Why not get married tomorrow?''

He eyed her uneasily.

''Oh,'' she spoke in a rush, ''I expect they want us really married before you leave.''

He shook his head. ''But we won't be. That is . . .'' He hesitated. ''You are too young to be left a widow. I'm not going to risk adding to your possible troubles by leaving you with a baby. We won't spend the night in the same bed.''

''Oh.'' Her cheeks turned hot and she could not bring herself to look at him. She was relieved.

The puppy bit her fingers. ''What is the puppy's name?'' she asked brightly.

''I didn't name him. I thought you would want to.''

The dog licked her hand, wagged his tail, and then cocked his head expectantly. She gave a shaky laugh.

''Jester. He makes me laugh so I will name him Jester.''

15 ❧ The Wedding

❧ Once when Faith had been very small she had gone berrying with Auntie Abbie. The raspberries near Auntie Abbie's house had not seemed as numerous as those on the other side of the fence, so Faith had climbed over the gate into the neighboring field. She had heard Auntie scream a warning just as she discovered a bull racing down the field toward her.

Those next few moments still stuck in her mind. She had run faster than she had known was possible. Her legs had hurt, her chest had hurt, and she had seen the field moving by her, but until Auntie Abbie had hauled her over the gate, all her effort had seemed in vain, for she had not been able to feel herself moving.

Her wedding gave her the same feeling. She could see things happening around her, she watched people talking with her, she listened to the ceremony, but she could not feel herself at all. Even when the sergeant, following the instructions of the Reverend Mr. Glover, had dutifully leaned over and kissed her cold cheek, her only feeling had been a faint surprise.

Not until it was over, not until she and Zachary were leaving Goody's house, saying good-bye, and thank you, did her usual feelings return to her. Then she remembered what Auntie Abbie had said after Faith had scrambled over the gate, dropped to the ground, and looked up to see the red eyes and flaring nostrils of the bull poking over the top of the gate. "Brave girl! A person who keeps going with as much determination as you do can handle whatever comes in life." After that Auntie Abbie had hugged her and burst into tears.

Now Goody was hugging her and Faith remembered the words. It was a long time since she had thought of that episode. She drew back from Goody and gave her a brilliant smile. She did not want to cry. She turned around to the clergyman and smiled blindly in his direction.

Then she turned around to Zachary Stedman and, taking his hand, tried to lead him out of Goody's house. He shook his head at her and politely thanked Goody and the clergyman for their efforts. Then he turned and headed back to the house. He gave her a quick glance and, in response to her eagerness to get away, hurried along so that she soon had to run to keep up with his long stride. By the time they reached the house, Faith was out of breath.

She stopped and looked around. Every time she saw the house she liked it more. The yellow stone of the doorstep was pleasant with the browned boards of the siding. It was a handsome building, positioned well; from the rooms inside one could look out over the valley. There was a door in the side of the house that opened onto a fenced yard and a path to the barn.

"I am the mistress of this house," announced Faith, a little astonished.

"Yes." Zachary Stedman swallowed hard. "Yes, you are indeed."

"I like it," Faith went on in a soft voice. "I like it better than any other house in Springfield. I like it better than any other house I've ever seen." She looked at him solemnly. "I'll take care of it as well as it can be taken care of."

"I . . . ah . . . yes."

He trailed her inside. There was a scratch at the door and he went to admit Jester. The puppy bounced into the keeping room and raced about.

"Jester has to behave himself in the house," announced Faith.

"I hope so," said the man dubiously.

Faith walked around the hearth and the rest of the keeping room with her eyes squinting as she considered it. She looked up and caught an expression on the sergeant's face that made her shy. It reminded her that although he was a stern man, he was also kind.

"Why weren't you already married?" she asked. "You have such a nice house, I would think you'd have wanted to share it."

"I'm not really sure. I missed Suzanna for a long time after she died. Since then, I have served as a guide much of the time. I haven't had the opportunity to get to know any young women."

"Do you miss your house when you are away from it?"

"I shall like knowing it will be well cared for," he said carefully. "Now you must be shown around." He went to the far end of the keeping room and took the lid off a barrel. "The wheat is stored in here." He showed her the contents of the other barrels. "Do you want to go to the attic and see the rest?"

"Not now. Later. Where did all your food come from?"

"Goody got a lot for me. When I have to be away I leave her with instructions."

She looked pleased. "I won't go hungry."

"No. Well, of course you might have people billeted here before I return."

"But there is so much!" She gave a contented sigh. "Did you want me to cook supper?"

"If you cook you may discover things you want to ask me about. You start supper and I will feed the animals. Then I will come in to see if you have found all you need."

He went outside. Faith was relieved. She hoped he would not come back inside soon because she felt self-conscious cooking in a new place. Although Auntie had taught her to cook well, she knew that only experience would make her adept at a strange hearth.

She moved back and forth setting out the knives and pots, choosing the foods she would cook with. It all seemed so unreal. The girl who had been Faith Ralston was now Mistress Zachary Stedman. Married — and to a man she hardly knew! She thought over all that had happened in the last month and shivered. She had to concentrate fiercely to get on with peeling the onions.

Two hours later she had a pigeon pie ready to eat. They began to eat in awkward silence. Some of the pie crust was almost uncooked and some was burnt, but there was still enough good pie to eat. She watched him anxiously.

"I think you have done well for the first time with this hearth," he finally said.

She nodded quickly. "It takes getting used to."

She sneaked a quick look at him and it occurred to her that he was shy. He was so competent and authoritative it had not occurred to her before that his stern manner might be an indication of shyness. It was a revelation that she stored away to think over when she was alone.

The evening passed rapidly, filled with instruction on how to care for the animals when they became snowbound. In addition to Jester and Blanche, there were two hogs, six chickens, and an old sheep to care for. "For wool," he explained. "I've had Blackie so long I'd rather hunt a deer than eat her."

She listened, surprised. She had thought he was too practical a man to allow himself to grow fond of a useful animal. There was evidently a lot about him that she did not know.

She helped him pack food for the long days on the trail. "Don't you hunt at all as you go along?" she asked.

"It wastes time that I may not have and it requires a fire that might be dangerous."

"When you are traveling around as a scout do you ever meet your friend Wannalancet?"

His face took on a grim look. "Since the war began I have tried not to. Wannalancet is not a Christian Indian. He is now on the enemy side."

She shivered. "But what will you do if he tries to kill you?"

Shocked, he said, "He would not."

She persisted. "What if he tried to kill some colonist and you were watching?"

"I hope that will never happen."

She opened her mouth to pursue the subject, but the misery on his face kept her quiet.

Long into the night they burned rushlights while he finished his preparations. Finally he said, "Time for sleep. I'll lie down before the hearth. I'll be as happy there as I would be in the bedstead."

The high bedstead was piled with blankets and comforters, and there was even a pillow. Faith ran her hand over a plaided red and blue pattern. "Where did you get such nice blankets?"

"I barter with furs. I trapped for six winters to earn this house and all that you see in it." There was pride in his voice.

"Did . . . did Suzanna make any of these blankets?"

"Suzanna? She made a dark blue and white blanket. It is in the chest."

"Oh." Faith was glad it was not on the bed.

He looked awkward. "Sleep well."

The door closed. She could hear him stirring in the keeping room and then all was silent. She undressed quickly and slipped a wool nightshirt over her head. The bed creaked as she climbed in and creaked with every move she made. She leaned over and carefully blew out the rushlight. The comforters settled around her warmly.

Wind stirred in the pines by the lane. In the distance a fox barked. Inside the house all was quiet. At first she had been relieved when Zachary said he would not sleep with her. She had taken his decision as an indication of his kindness and thoughtfulness. But maybe he didn't want to sleep with her because he found her displeasing. Maybe he thought her too skinny. She ran her hand down over her body. She had so many bones sticking out and so few soft curves.

He had not wanted to marry, he said so himself. Tears began to wet her cheeks. She wished he would come to the bed, even if only for company. She would like having him for company and warmth. If only . . . but sleep won out.

Morning, as always, was cold. She thought she had awakened early, but already there were noises from the keeping room. She could hear the puppy whining at the door.

She hurried into her garments. Her hair finally in its neat plait, she entered the keeping room. Evidently

Zachary was now out in the barn. The fire had been stirred and water was heating. She put a pot of porridge over the coals and set the table.

"That smells good." Zachary came in with Jester. The puppy raced around and around, returning repeatedly to Faith for a pat.

"He almost made a breakfast of one of the chickens." Zachary frowned. "He will have to be watched carefully while he is young." He found a hunk of stale bread and tossed it to the puppy. Jester settled down and began to chew happily. He wagged his tail when he saw he was being watched.

Faith giggled. "He's funny."

As soon as breakfast was over Zachary fastened his pack on his back. He hesitated uneasily in the doorway.

"I may not be back until springtime."

"Do you really have to go? Haven't you done your share?"

His face set in stern lines. "No one has just a share. Things are far too bad for that, Faith. Unless every man does all he can, experiences like yours will happen again and again."

"I hope you kill every Indian you find," she said with a viciousness that surprised her.

"I will kill when I must. The Indians are fighting for their lives so they are very dangerous, but they are still human beings."

"It's difficult to remember that when I think about the massacre."

"Some of the colonists have done things just as horrible to the Indians. So much damage has been done that the war may be over soon. Neither we nor the Indians have the resources to keep on as we have been.''

''No,'' said Faith.

''Well, good-bye.''

Faith was suddenly very afraid to have him leave. ''Be . . . be very careful.''

His smile was unexpectedly sweet. ''My Indian friends say I am as slippery as a fish. Don't worry about me.''

He stepped out the door and looked back uncertainly. She was filled with the pain of loss. She gasped and stepped after him. Grabbing his jerkin tightly, she went up on tiptoe to kiss him on the lips. Instantly his arms went around her, holding her so tightly that she hurt.

The kiss lasted a long time before he stepped back. She could see he was breathing in short gasps. His weather-beaten skin flushed red. He gave a stiff nod and turned away.

He hurried down the path to the road that traveled north. Even before he was out of sight he settled into a fast, regular pace that was more rapid than he had used on their trek from High Hills to Springfield. Faith walked to the edge of the hill and watched him go; it didn't take long for him to disappear. He did not turn to wave.

16 ❧ Peter

❧ Winter was losing its fierce grip on the land but the snow was still deep. Goody had said that there might be snowstorms into April, but on this pleasant February afternoon that was difficult to believe. While Faith stood at the well lowering the bucket with the help of the creaking wellsweep, she wore only a shawl yet was comfortable in the warm rays of the sun.

She always found this view of the valley impressive. Although the house was not very far from the green by which so many other homes were clustered, it was placed uphill and set at an angle away from the lane. From the yard between the house and the barn one could see over the river to the far valley and to the spread of hills beyond. The road north, where she had last seen Zachary, curved around the hill not far below the house.

Faith noticed now that someone was walking along that road. The figure was just far enough away so that she could not see it clearly, yet there was enough shape and flutter to it that she guessed it was a woman. Another person followed close behind. The second figure, tall and thin, seemed more like a man.

Faith stopped lowering the bucket to watch them, for she eagerly anticipated Zachary's return. For her he symbolized security and safety in a world that still terrified her. Whenever her memories plagued her, she could control them by recalling his firm voice, his steady gray eyes, and the strength of his broad shoulders. She had not seen him since the morning after their wedding, exactly three months ago. They were married on November 16 and today was February 16.

Through the long winter days, through the hours of weaving and the spinning that Goody had taught her, she had a lot of time to think about him. At first she thought mostly about how grateful she was to Zachary for her home.

The more she thought about it, the prouder she was that she had been left in charge of all these possessions. It pleased her to keep the house clean. Sometimes as she swept or scrubbed she dwelt on the memory of the kiss he had given her when they said good-bye. She wondered what he thought of her.

She got Goody to tell her as much about Zachary Stedman as she knew.

"To tell the truth, Faith, I don't know that much about Zachary's earliest days," Goody had said, looking puzzled. "Maybe someday you can get him to talk about them. When he arrived here about ten years ago — seventeen he was — he came with one of the old trappers. Ranulf took to him right away, but Suzanna wasn't much impressed at first. Zachary is a real quiet man, you know, but he was even more so in those days. He's warmed up, though he never has talked much. Talks more with you than I ever known him to do before, even in the days when he was planning to marry Suzanna.''

That thought stayed with Faith and cheered her. Maybe she was special to Zachary. Maybe he could be happy he married her. If he remained stern and silent, what would it be like to live with him all the time? What would the intimacy of being man and wife be like for Zachary and her?

Now she squinted in hopes of getting a better view of the people on the road. She did not think the man was Zachary. He was more likely to come through the forest, alone. Someday she would turn around and he would be standing there, looking at her with his deepset gray eyes.

News from the surrounding towns had been bad all winter. Indians had attacked one community after another. Faith tried not to listen to the terrifying reports. Sometimes she was able to talk about the massacre, but only with Goody, who was calm and comforting. Most other people, talkative and fearful, made her want to scream at them to leave her alone. Twice she had let herself be convinced to stay in the garrison overnight. The crush of people, the fear — so intense it could almost be touched — made her memories of the massacre unbearably strong.

This being washday, she put thoughts of new arrivals

and Indians out of her mind and busied herself. When she spent time doing household tasks — washing, cleaning, polishing — the unpleasant things of life got pushed away. It made the threat of the Indians seem less real.

As she staggered from the well toward the keeping room with her fourth bucketful of water, Jester dashed around the corner of the house and headed for the lane in such a hurry that he almost knocked her down. "Stupid dog," she scolded. Jester had a loud, piercing yip when something captured his attention. Now he stood in the middle of West Lane with his legs spread apart, yipping for all he was worth. Faith set down her bucket and went to see what was causing his excitement.

From the street there was a clear view down to the village green. The two arrivals were there with Mr. Glover, so easy to identify by his height. She identified Goody by her bulk, and many more. Curiosity led her down the hill.

Many in the gathering noticed her coming and turned toward her expectantly. The man who had arrived was so tall that he stood head and shoulders above everyone but the clergyman. He had a familiar air but she could not immediately identify him. It was not until he faced her directly that she saw the bulbous eyes and the convulsive lump in his throat.

"Peter! Is it you?"

She stood as if rooted. It was Peter — taller, broader of shoulder, and heavier boned, although the flesh on those bones seemed scarce enough. He had lost the look of being a skinny youth and now, hardly four months later, he was a tall, somewhat scrawny young man. To see him alive and well — the tears seemed to come from the soles of her feet. She could only stand, the tears running freely down her cheeks, repeating, "Peter, Peter, Peter!"

He stood and grinned at her, nodding. "Aye, it's me, right enough."

Goody said, "He tells us that the Indians who carried out the massacre at High Hills were Narragansetts. They wasted no time in herding their prisoners from High Hills all the way up to Canada."

"To Canada? All of you, Peter? Even little Betty?"

He nodded quickly. "All of us . . . at least most of us that started made it. Up to Montreal, Faith. I was lucky. I no sooner got there than a man from Boston paid to have me sent home."

"What about Mistress Keene?" Her voice cracked.

He stopped nodding and his grin left. "Oh, Faith, she couldn't make it. She fell down on the trail so they killed her."

Faith shuddered. The rest stood in respectful silence. Faith opened her mouth to ask for details. She decided she did not want them.

Peter took a deep breath and went on. "The Keene twins, though; despite everything, they're fine. They are up in Canada and not likely to come home. They've been taken in by a French farmer's family and seem to like it well enough. I don't know about Ralph. He did not get taken north with us and I was so confused while the Indians were attacking that I didn't see what happened to him.''

Faith looked away. ''He's dead.''

Peter swallowed hard. ''The other women managed well enough on the trail — Mistress Sedgewick, Goodwife Young, and Goodwife Brown. I think that Mistress Sedgewick and Goodwife Brown are on their way home now.''

''I'm so glad,'' said Faith softly. ''I worried about them, about Mistress Sedgewick especially. You know that all their husbands . . .''

''I know,'' said Peter grimly. ''I saw all that before we were taken off. Your father, too. Yes, I saw it all. But he did not suffer long, Faith.''

Faith wiped her eyes. ''Peter, do you know what happened to the Brown boys?''

''They're coming home with their mother. The youngest one became very ill on the march. I didn't think he'd make it, but all those Browns are a determined lot. He's all right now.''

After a pause Goody said, ''This is Mistress Palmer. Your friend Peter brought her down from Northampton. She had her house burned but she escaped. Peter met Mistress Palmer's husband and children in Canada. Master Palmer asked Peter to fetch Mistress Palmer and bring her down here to her sister's. They did not know that her sister had . . .'' Goody paused. ''That her sister died in the fire in October here. So, she needs a place to stay.''

Faith nodded gravely toward the unknown face in the crowd.

Mistress Palmer stared back suspiciously. She was an unappealing woman, short and broad hipped, with a drawn look to her long face. Eyes like black currants gazed resentfully at the world. An odor of sickness hung about her, acrid and penetrating.

Mr. Glover's voice was hearty. "We will allow you the privilege of housing our needy guests, Mistress Stedman. Yours is the house most suitable for them now, I believe."

Faith tried to smile, but failed. She was glad to see Peter but she had enjoyed living alone. Living by herself she could control the daily rituals of housework, regular duties which she performed with religious care and which helped her pretend that she had some control over her life.

It was true, however, that every other household was keeping a stranger or even, in some cases, an entire family of strangers. As the war progressed, more and more of the homeless drifted into the town or were brought there by militiamen for care. Faith knew it was only fair for her to start providing shelter and food for those in need. If she did not, Peter and Mistress Palmer would probably have to live in the garrison. Truly, she could not wish that on anyone.

She nodded and tried to lie politely. "I will be pleased to do what I can."

Peter suddenly grinned. "I'm glad we'll be staying with you, Faith. You make good porridge."

Faith was astonished. This new Peter was very different from the old. The old Peter used to be too shy to speak in front of so many others. Evidently he had grown in more than breadth and height. She wondered if he ever felt the cold and the screaming inside as she did. She wondered if he ever felt, as she did, such panic that words would not come.

Mistress Palmer grunted and said, "You came down from uphill. Your house ain't in the middle of things. I don't like not being close in."

She looked around the circle but no one answered her. The clergyman frowned.

"I'll go back home and start preparing things," said Faith. She hurried up the hill, hiding her face as she went so that no one would see her crying.

By the time she reached the house she had command of herself again. She wiped her eyes fiercely and pulled out bedding. She hoped Peter would tell her about his trip to Canada and back. Actually, it might be rather comforting to have Peter around, but she dreaded the presence of the woman.

"This is a wonderful house," said Peter a short time later as he looked around, impressed. "I praise the Lord that you didn't get captured, Faith. I was hoping you could stay hidden. You would have been cold and hungry and have suffered so."

A shudder passed through him and he turned to peer out of a window. "I would never have guessed the sergeant would have a house like this. He was almost like an Indian. How did you come to marry him, Faith?"

Mistress Palmer looked up, her eyes narrowed. "Sergeant Stedman, the scout?" She looked around, her nose twitching. "So! This is his house, eh?" She nodded wisely. "Not for long, I'm thinking."

Faith paled. Peter frowned. "What do you mean by that?" he asked.

Mistress Palmer smirked and shrugged her shoulders. "He's enemy, that's what. Or at least as good as enemy. Injun lover, he is, I've heard tell. Got real mad at Captain Mosely, he did, because the captain shot those Christian Injuns in Marlborough. Called what Mosely did an outrage. Yelled at Mosely's men — told them they were getting what they deserved if the Injuns scalped them."

She smirked at the startled expressions on their faces. "You can't treat the Injuns like people. They're devils, they be. Mosely knows that. Stedman — his best friend is an Injun. Man like that, his own kind can't trust him."

"Anyone can trust him," said Faith fiercely, although her voice trembled a bit. "He's a good man."

The woman spat into the corner. "He's a fool, he is." She picked up one of the fine pewter candlesticks and set it down again. "Folks will take this house from him soon, no doubt about that. If I was you, miss, I'd leave while the going is good."

"No." Faith glared at the woman. "This is my home and I'm staying here."

Mistress Palmer shrugged her bony shoulders and went on poking and prying. Faith began to heat up porridge. She trembled with so much rage that she found it difficult to work.

She almost forgot about Mistress Palmer while Peter told her of the march to Canada. Peter was not a good storyteller, but even so Faith could picture the scene: the confusion, the desperation, and the terror that the captives felt as, wounded and stunned, they were herded away. She could easily imagine the feeling of walking long days in the cold, hungry, with sore feet, knowing that if she lagged she would be killed. Then the nights of sleeping on the ground without cover.

"Mistress Keene was the one that surprised me," he said. "You know how she was forever fussing. Well, she just wouldn't let anyone fuss for fear it would irritate the Indians. She somehow calmed everyone down and made us all behave so that we wouldn't antagonize the Indians."

His voice shook as he went on. Suddenly he broke down and cried with great gasps, burying his face in his hands. "It was terrible, Faith, terrible," he said when he finally gained control. "Poor Mistress Keene, none of her efforts helped her. They just tomahawked her when she got weak. She died so bravely, Faith. She was a brave woman and her faith was a great support to her."

Somehow Faith wasn't surprised. Those who had strong faith seemed better able to face terrors. "I'm glad for her," she said softly. "Oh, Peter, I am so confused, but I hope that someday I will have a faith that can serve me as well." She thought about Mistress Keene as she cried, but the tears were healing and she was finally able to smile at Peter again.

"Little Betty?" she asked. "I remember hearing her cry."

His face lightened. "Everyone loves Betty, even the Indian who owned her. He carried her on his shoulders when she got tired." He shook his head. "I don't think she'll come back. She likes Montreal. The nuns take care of her and she told me that she likes them too much to leave. She wants to stay. They made her a pretty dress."

"Nuns?"

"The French in Canada are Catholic and there were nuns where we were taken by the Indians to be sold. The French hate the English so much that they enjoy having us as servants. After the French paid the Indians for us the women got placed in French homes as household servants and most of the boys did too, but the girls were sent to live with the nuns."

Faith tried to imagine what it must be like. "What about Goodwife Young? She took good care of Betty and loved her as if she were her own child. Where was she?"

"I didn't get a chance to talk with her. She got sent off right away. We've heard tell that she's supervising the dairy women at a big farm. It's a lot better being with the French than with Indians, but she's still a prisoner. They probably don't let her see Betty."

"But, Peter, why isn't she coming home?"

"Each person has to be negotiated for. I was lucky." He grinned ruefully. "Men tend to make trouble. Maybe that's why they were glad to get rid of me."

"Goodwife Young is obviously a very capable woman.

I suppose the French would want her to stay if they could get her to."

"I was told it might be years before everybody can be gotten out," said Peter sadly. "I pray for them daily."

"As will I," said Faith.

After eating, Faith began to prepare a bed for Peter in the loft.

"I'll sleep with you in the bedstead," announced Mistress Palmer. "I have aching in my joints and I must sleep off the floor."

Faith gritted her teeth. "My husband is due back any time now," she answered. "He will sleep with me as soon as he comes. You may sleep on a pallet in front of the fire. It will stay warm and comfortable there all night. If you don't want that, we will fix you a bed of leaves in the loft."

"I can't climb up to the loft!" exclaimed the woman, glaring.

"You will find the pallet warm and comfortable, I am sure," said Faith firmly.

Mistress Palmer pointedly turned her back on Faith. Peter grinned when his eyes met Faith's, and it warmed her. It was so good to have a friend. She could not remember when she had felt so happy. Not only had she managed to be forceful, but wasn't it amazing how Peter had changed! She had not thought it possible that being captured by Indians could be good for anyone, but it had certainly strengthened Peter.

17 ⚐ *The Dismal Time*

⚐ The long-time colonists kept exclaiming over the mild March weather. "Never known it this warm in March," repeated Goody every time Faith saw her. "Won't last though. The spring storms I've known! Five feet of snow once — and that after the fruit trees had blossomed."

But no snow fell, and despite the hefty gusts of wind that often came, the house was soon warm enough to bank the fire for part of the day.

Of course, Mistress Palmer complained when Faith banked the fire. "I get real cold," she fussed, hunching her shoulders until she looked like a defenseless weasel. "I ain't young and energetic like you."

"It would be good for you to get up and move about more," Faith pointed out. "You could do some sweeping; that is warming."

Mistress Palmer sulked. "I ain't bin well."

Faith bit her tongue. She did not believe the woman

was as ill as she claimed. She spent her mornings hanging over the fire, asking Peter or Faith to fetch whatever she wanted because she was "that weary." Every noon she walked down into town and gossiped with whomever she found. Faith almost felt guilty that she could find nothing about Mistress Palmer to like and so much to dislike.

Peter, however, was a pleasure to have around. He had become a lot like Papa. As time went on, Faith had begun to imagine that she had really been very fond of Papa. So when Peter started talking in the pious way that used to annoy her, she only regarded him with a resigned, fond amusement.

Surprisingly, Peter turned out to be handy. Not only had he gained strength during his time in Canada, but he had become less awkward. He chopped wood, made repairs, and fashioned a couple of stools for the table.

It was old Master Floyd who brought them the news about Master Palmer. The old man was fond of Peter and often stopped by to talk with him. He waited until after lunch when Mistress Palmer left the house before he spoke.

"Heard 'em talking down ta green," he announced. " 'Twas a militiaman from Northfield come by. He says Palmer got wounded on the way back from Canada and they're going to bring him down here as soon as possible. Folks think his wife ought to be doing the nursing."

Two days later when Master Palmer arrived, Faith could not help but be sorry for him. "He's so weak," she whispered to Peter. "Do you think he's going to die?"

"Only good men die." Peter's cynicism shocked her. At her wide-eyed stare he shrugged. "Sick as he is, he eyes this house in the same way his wife does. You know — as if he's deciding how he wants things once he gets rid of you."

"Oh. I thought I was imagining that."

Peter sighed. "The Bible warns us in Timothy that the evil man shall wax worse and worse, deceiving and being deceived. It also says that a good Christian should be long-suffering and patient. It's going to be difficult to be patient with those Palmers." He sighed again. "But I'll try."

William Palmer was better-fleshed than his wife. His wound had come from an arrowhead that had ripped into a muscle and caused infection. Being such a large and very ill man he created a lot of work but, much to Faith's relief, he did express gratefulness for their efforts and seldom complained as his wife did. Faith found she did not mind his presence as much as she had expected.

Nonetheless, Faith continued struggling to overcome her dislike of the Palmers. She tried to convince herself that they had suffered and needed special understanding. But so many others had suffered, were suffering even worse and bearing it better, that thinking about it only made her dislike them more. She was finally driven to ask Peter to recommend scripture that might help.

Peter was only too willing to instruct her. "Do you remember that, in one of his sermons, Mr. Glover said that we are all being punished for the way we have lived? He quoted to us, 'I will give them into the hands of their enemies, and into the hand of them that seek their life and their dead bodies shall be meat to the fowls of heaven, and to the beasts of the earth.' He also quoted, 'And instead of a sweet smell there shall be a stink.' That reminds me for certain of having Mistress Palmer in the house.''

Faith giggled.

''And, oh, Faith, I have such fear because he quoted, 'Thy men shall fall by the sword and thy Mighty by the War.' ''

This depressing information weighed down Faith for hours until she settled down with Zachary's Bible and started looking through it herself.

''Ha,'' she said to Peter and made him come over to follow the words as she read aloud: '' 'The Lord was gracious to them, and had compassion on them, and had respect unto them, and would not destroy them, neither cast from them his presence as yet.'

''See? The Bible can be helpful, Peter. And look at this from Isaiah. It says 'That war against thee shall be as nothing, and as a thing of naught.' ''

She closed the big book reverently. ''The word of the Lord can reassure, Peter. Mr. Glover is just gloomy from all the war, like the Reverend Mr. Mather.''

Peter looked puzzled. ''I tell you, Faith, it seems to me like a punishment to have the Palmers here. I tell you what I'll do: the next time she fusses at one of us I'll just think of her being a 'thing of naught.' That might make it easier for me to hold my tongue.''

Faith giggled again and felt a bit more cheerful. ''I

just pretend I don't notice when she's glaring at me,'' she said.

Faith had to pretend not to notice a lot in the next few days. She was often aware of an abrupt halt in conversation when she came near the Palmers. Then there was their attempt to get Peter to think ill of Faith by criticizing her cooking.

Peter was astounded by their attitude. ''Faith's a fine cook,'' he asserted, surprised that anyone doubted it. ''Hers is perhaps the best cooking in the village. Even my mam couldn't do up a stew as tasty, especially considering the short commons. And she never — well, almost never — burns the porridge.''

As for Beatrix Palmer's spiteful comments about pasty-faced girls, he replied, truly astonished, ''But Faith is surely the prettiest girl in Springfield. Not only is she pretty, but she's graceful and her voice is nice to listen to.''

The more Peter supported her, the warmer Faith felt toward him. No one had ever praised her appearance before. Certainly Papa had not. Auntie Abbie had been convinced that praising a girl's appearance led to vanity. ''Handsome is as handsome does,'' had been her invariable comment when Faith had presented herself for approval. Even when Faith, dressed in her best, pressed her for further comment, she would only say, ''You'll do.''

Peter's comments made her feel good. She realized she felt better about herself when Peter was around. Soon Peter himself looked good to her. Instead of the ungainly length of his arms, she noticed their strength.

Instead of the bulging of his pale eyes, she noticed their gaze of concern for her.

Papa had approved of Peter and Peter had greatly admired Papa. Given just the merest suggestion of interest in Papa, Peter would talk of him endlessly.

"He was one who inspired others," he would say enthusiastically to a bored William Palmer. "A man of great depth and courage, a man who knew his God." He shook his head in wonder. "Master Ralston could quote scripture like no one else I've ever met. And pray? Ah, he prayed so that he brought his hearers truly to the throne of God."

"A preacher?" asked William Palmer.

"Not a clergyman, but truly a great believer. Heaven is fortunate in his presence."

Beatrix Palmer would eye Faith slyly. "Daughter ain't much like him seems."

Peter himself could not appreciate Faith's private religious devotion, since he, as Papa had been, was more inclined to a piety zealous enough to appear sanctimonious. Nonetheless, loyalty made him protest. "She has much of his strength of character. He was proud of her, I'm sure of that. A hard worker, Faith is. A father would have nothing to complain about."

Whenever Peter praised Faith he smiled at her and she smiled back. As time went on, it became harder to smile. How was she going to get the Palmers to leave?

It became a very rainy spring. The lanes went from being bothersomely slippery to impassably muddy. Word trickled back of disastrous Indian attacks at Rehoboth and Providence. Faith caught Peter's cold. Mold formed on the last of the flour. Faith heard the sound of rain on the roof as she fell asleep. She awoke to the sound of steady dripping from the eaves.

Even Jester got depressed. He curled up in a corner of the keeping room, looking miserable.

"I know how you feel," Faith whispered to him, scratching his ears. "If I had a tail I'm sure it would be drooping, too."

18 ❧ Waiting

❧ Faith leaned over and picked up another twig. Absently she broke it in half and piled it on the rest of her load. She shivered. She was not far from the open yard where sunlight made a pool of warmth, but here under the trees it was chilly.

Mayflowers bloomed among the rotting oak leaves, the wee pink blossoms giving the spot a sweet delicious fragrance. Flowers already and the sergeant still not home! She stood and peered through the bare branches of the trees off into the valley below. If only he would come.

"He's bound to be dead." William Palmer had been repeating this refrain a lot recently. Since last November, when the sergeant had left, there had been no message from him and no word about him from anyone else. Information about other militiamen came from here and there. It was now April and no one had seen or heard of Sergeant Zachary Stedman.

"Of course, he's a scout," Peter often pointed out. "Scouts don't fight like militiamen do. They work best when they can't be traced." His voice was always carefully hopeful. He didn't like upsetting Faith.

Faith shut her eyes tightly and leaned against the rough bark of an oak. She did not want to give up hope. Papa had become difficult to visualize. Even the memory of Auntie Abbie was sliding away. Life in Springfield was so vastly different from the calm, ordered existence of Auntie's Sussex home that it was hard to believe that such a life had ever existed.

Zachary Stedman's face would not form before her, but she often recalled his strong shoulders and arms as he worked that day when he dug the graves at High Hills. She remembered the tone of his voice when he told her she must read the scripture to honor the dead. His voice had been firm at a time when her mind was seething with terrifying images and she could not shape words. Most of all, she remembered the feeling of security she had felt when she was with him.

She sighed. Peter was a pleasanter companion than anyone else now available, but she could not say she felt secure in his presence.

"Faith, Faith."

She sighed again. That deep bellow belonged to Peter. Back in the days aboard ship Peter's voice had cracked now and then. No longer; now it was deep and loud. Faith picked up her twigs and started back to the house.

"There you are." Peter sounded relieved. "I came

back to find the fire almost out and no one in the house. Where are the Palmers?''

Faith peered inside. "I don't know. They were here when I left. He has been moving about a bit more recently. Maybe he decided to walk to the green.''

"Good," said Peter. "The more they can keep out of the house the better I'll like it. Oh, Faith, you don't have to fix the fire. I can do it.''

He leaned over the hearth as she came up and their heads collided with a resounding crack. "Ow!" she exclaimed, pressing on her scalp to relieve the pain.

"Did I hurt you?" Peter asked, looking at her mournfully. "I'm sorry, Faith.''

He put his hand out awkwardly and gently touched the side of her head.

She gave a hiccupy laugh. "It will be better in a minute.''

His hand, unexpectedly gentle, smoothed the soft hair at her brow where the tendrils broke free.

"Peter?''

"I never want to see you hurt," he whispered. "You are so pretty, Faith.''

For a long moment they stared at each other. The angled afternoon sunlight streamed in through the window and broke up the dimness of the room, illuminating the fuzz over Peter's upper lip, lightening the blue of his eyes. There was a matching blue vein that ran from the edge of his eyes onto his cheek, which showed clearly in the sunlight.

Faith's lips parted and she swayed forward. Peter leaned over and his soft full lips met hers and drew back. She smiled up at him questioningly. Had he meant to kiss her? It was a short kiss. It wasn't at all like the one Zachary had given her.

Peter's large eyes filled with tears. He looked solemnly down on her. "I should not have kissed you," he said wretchedly. "You are a married lady. That was a sin on my part."

For a moment Faith was startled by how much Peter reminded her of Papa. That somehow made her feel as if she were doing the right thing to kiss Peter. She felt less lonely.

She looked down. "I wonder if I am a married lady. The sergeant disappeared five months ago, Peter. He's probably dead."

"If he is," Peter warned, "you may lose this house to the Palmers. They certainly are working to take it away from you. I thought, Faith, that if you could pretend to be in the family way you might be able to keep the house."

"What do you mean? Pretend to have a baby? I can't do that, Peter. If I were going to have the sergeant's baby it would be showing on me by now."

Peter knelt again at the fire, his face turned away from her. "If he's dead you could marry me, Faith. I could give you a baby and then you wouldn't have to worry about losing the house."

Faith stared in astonishment at the back of Peter's head. He must be very worried to make such a suggestion. She walked slowly to the door and stared into the afternoon sunshine. It terrified her to think of losing the house.

"Do you know what the Palmers are saying, Peter?"

Peter's voice was strained. "Goody is very worried. She told me that the Palmers went to the Reverend Mr. Glover to complain about the sergeant being an Indian-lover. They told him what they told us — that the sergeant says much of our suffering is the result of colonists behaving toward Indians with pointless cruelty."

"And what did Mr. Glover say?"

"He told Goody that unfortunately the sergeant is known to have argued with a clergyman who claimed that the Indians were demons. The sergeant claimed that the Indians were just very resentful humans. Did you know, Faith, that the sergeant is a friend of the Reverend John Eliot, who is an apostle to the Indians?

"Anyway, Mr. Glover didn't tell that to the Palmers. Instead, he told them that he had never doubted the sergeant's loyalty to his own people. He also told them that it would be sinful to spread stories about the sergeant while you are unprotected by his presence."

"But of course they go on spreading such stories around."

Peter shrugged.

"What else did Goody say?"

"She said there is a lot of sentiment against the sergeant. So much so, that if the Palmers made a fuss in public meeting, she and the Reverend Mr. Glover might not be able to protect your ownership of the house."

Faith looked wildly from Peter's face to the fire and around the room. Where was the sergeant? Why hadn't he sent a message so that she would at least know he was alive? She gripped her hands together and tried to tell herself not to be so terrified.

She licked her lips. "Peter, did Goody suggest what you mentioned . . . you know, getting me with a baby?"

He shook his head quickly. "I didn't mention that to Goody." He sounded appalled.

"I'm going to go right now to talk with Goody myself," said Faith. "You'd better come along, Peter. If you are going to be of any help to me you had better help decide what I should do."

Goody was not able to offer any help. As for Peter's idea, she snorted when she heard it. "No clergyman will marry the two of you yet, methinks. Not until more time has gone by. And fair and afar off you be if you think compassion will make folks determine to let you keep the house just because you have a babe coming. Might do, but just as likely, they might take it away from you for bad behavior. Patience, patience. We may get a message from Zachary in the next few days." She hugged Faith. "Remember, child: 'All things work together for good to them that love God.' "

Faith walked back to the house glumly and Peter stomped after her, even more despondent. Rachel Fitch, a girl of Faith's age, whose father had been killed early in the winter, gave Peter a saucy look as they passed. Faith looked back after they passed and caught Rachel looking after them with yearning. Faith turned then to

Peter to see what attracted Rachel. With a sharply critical gaze she saw him as a gangly, pale youth, beginning to fill out well, but awkward and stooped. It would be difficult for anyone to praise his appearance. He could not begin to compare with Zachary.

Appearance did not really matter, she told herself sternly. What really mattered in a person was character and ability. She should not compare Peter to Zachary. Zachary was more than ten years older and braver, she was certain, than most men could ever be. According to Goody, lots of women were interested in Zachary but he had taken a long time to get over missing Suzanna.

If she were left with only Peter . . . well, she was fond of Peter. And she was very fond of the house.

The Palmers were still out. Faith began to busy herself with the evening meal. Peter stood around, darting looks at her that were half sheepish, half guilty, as if he were a naughty puppy.

Finally she turned and snapped at him. "It really is time for feeding the beasts, Peter. You might make yourself useful."

His shoulders more hunched than ever, he disappeared in the direction of the barn.

She bent over the hearth, stirring the grains she was slowly roasting over the open fire. The late afternoon light was suddenly blocked from the open doorway. She looked up to see a figure standing there, but the light shone in so that she had to squint to identify it.

"Good day, Faith." The deep-timbred voice was very familiar.

"It's you!" Grain scattered into the fire as she jumped to her feet.

He stepped all the way inside and she saw him well. Now she could see the strain of his last months. He was leaner than ever; it looked as if he must have gone hungry often. The deepset gray eyes were more sunken in their sockets and his hair was longer. Lines were deeply etched around his eyes and nose. These signs of his suffering shocked her and she began to cry.

He looked bewildered. "Did I frighten you?"

She nodded and whispered, "I had begun to think you weren't coming back." She went closer and touched his arm. "It's hard to believe you are real."

He smiled the softest smile she had ever seen on his face.

"I'm glad to be back," he said.

As he spoke there were steps outside the door. A querulous voice made him look up and draw back from her. The Palmers walked in.

19 ❧ *The Return*

❧ "I smell burning wheat," said Beatrix Palmer, stepping into the keeping room ahead of her husband. "Won't do to be careless, girl. There's not much of that wheat left."

As the woman moved forward she noticed the stranger in the room. "Come, girl. Entertaining when it's time for fixing the meal?"

Faith looked at her angrily. Beatrix Palmer was getting bossier every day and, despite Faith's antagonism, was treating her more and more like a servant.

The silence drew out.

Finally the sergeant spoke. "I have never met these people, Faith."

Peter came in with a full bucket of milk. "Sergeant! Sergeant Stedman! Are we glad to see you, sir."

"And I you, Peter." He looked at the Palmers. "How many people are living here?"

Faith, enjoying the dumbfounded expression of the

Palmers, was at last able to speak. "Only three in addition to me. These people are the Palmers. Peter and Mistress Palmer arrived in February and Master Palmer arrived about four weeks later."

"We've been real sick, Sergeant," explained Beatrix Palmer. "I got real affected by being took to Canada and Will here was got in the leg by an Indian arrow."

"One of Captain Turner's men?"

"Aye, sir."

The sergeant nodded.

Peter could keep still no longer. "We've been so worried — no one knew anything at all about you. Faith feared you were dead."

"I've been all over, but few have seen me. I report mostly to Captain Turner."

William Palmer looked excited. "I hear he's been on the attack."

The sergeant nodded. "I think Turner has done it — turned the tide. With his most recent attack and with the entrance of the Mohawks to help us out, it won't be long to the end now."

"We've won the war?" asked Peter, his voice loud with excitement.

The sergeant's face looked more drained than ever. "No one is going to win this war. It will end when the Indians are so weak that not a one of them can fight. We're almost there now."

"Can you stay home now?" Faith was afraid to hear the answer.

"That depends on the events of the next few weeks.

I'll stay for a while, anyway. I need some rest and I'd like to get some planting done. I'm not needed now as much as I was.'' He sat down on the stool that Peter pulled out for him by the hearth. ''I am glad you have been here to give Faith support,'' he said to Peter. ''I did not think it was good for her to be all alone for the whole winter. I expected Goody would get someone to live with her but I did not know who I would find here.''

Peter glowed with pleasure at the sergeant's words. It seemed that he already looked up to the sergeant the way he had once looked up to Papa.

''We have also been helping Faith,'' said William Palmer in an unctuous tone. ''My wife has been here longer than I have, and such a help she has been to a young girl with the work and also, of course, as a chaperone.''

Faith became vicious with her chopping of an onion and glared.

Peter looked astonished. ''But your wife hasn't helped Faith! All she has done is complain while Faith does all the cooking and cleaning for us.''

The pause after this statement seemed to bring Beatrix Palmer to her senses and she stepped over to Faith. ''Now I'll just finish that chopping while you visit with the sergeant,'' she said in a motherly fashion.

''No, ma'am,'' answered Faith, wielding her knife energetically. ''We will go on as we have been doing. If you truly wish to help you'll bring down the trenchers. I think the sergeant is more interested in food than in talk right now.''

The older woman sank down on a stool with a weary sigh. "I still get tuckered out from the least effort," she announced dramatically to the room at large. "When your heart's broke, your body just don't pull together as fast as it might." She sighed again. "You may not know, Sergeant Stedman, but I was marched to Canada with my two children and they were taken from me there."

"Ah, yes," said the sergeant. "I heard that they were there."

William Palmer looked up quickly. "Who was talking about them?"

"Goodman Pease. He says your children refused to return with you."

Beatrix Palmer hissed. "He went about it all wrong. They were tired and scared of the walk home. You don't ask young 'uns what they want to do, you tell them."

"They claimed you beat them."

"Of course I did," said William Palmer. "Any good parent beats children to make them behave."

The sergeant said nothing more. The Palmers fell into a sulky silence that lasted into the meal.

Faith listened contentedly as Peter told the story of his forced march. The sergeant watched him sympathetically. Faith felt proud of Peter. He had grown to be much more of a man in these last months. She wondered if he might ever grow to have that look of quiet authority that Zachary had.

After the meal Zachary nodded decisively at William Palmer. "Perhaps you can take some time before dark falls to do your packing," he suggested. "You'll stay here this night, of course, but on the morrow we will have a place for you to go. I'll see the Reverend Mr. Glover about it this evening."

"Not work!" exclaimed Beatrix Palmer, flabbergasted. "That ain't possible. I ain't well."

Zachary waved his hand at the emptied bowls. "You eat as well as a person in full health. I noticed you arrived here this afternoon with no sign of exhaustion. That is surprising after the climb up this hill. It would seem to me that you are in full enough health to work. Nothing too taxing, perhaps, but I'm sure there are households that need someone to do light jobs."

William Palmer ducked his head almost meekly. "I'm better, yes indeed," he agreed. "Not quite back to normal, of course, for that will take a few weeks yet, but I'm eager to start looking around."

"Something can be found for you, I'm sure," said Zachary.

"Soon, soon," agreed Palmer.

"Tomorrow," said Zachary.

Faith had to turn away to hide her relief.

The Palmers would have ventured out again that evening but for the thunderstorm that rolled in across the hills. Crack after crack of thunder reverberated overhead, rumbling away into the valley. Rain lashed against the clapboards and beat upon the shingles. Vagrant drafts made the rushlights flicker more erratically than usual.

Zachary said, "No point to keeping the lights lit. Might as well go to bed."

It amused Faith that they all followed his example without question. Zachary followed Faith into the parlor. \ "I sleep in the bedstead," she whispered. "I wouldn't let them put me out of it. Like the cooking, you see. If she took it over I thought she would take over the house."

Through the noise of the storm his voice was a comforting rumble. "You have done well. They have posed a great problem for you, I can see."

She was eager to explain herself. She stepped closer to him in order to see his face in the murky darkness. Close up he smelled of pine and the woodland floor. "Oh, yes. You see, I was afraid you had died because no one knew anything about you. None of the militiamen who came back could tell me anything. They were bad-talking you, the Palmers were. They have been trying to get folks against me by saying you are an Indian-lover."

His tone became very bitter. "No one will call me an Indian-lover now. In the most recent raid I killed three Indians — all of them had been friends of mine. They were attacking a household along the river."

At her shocked gasp he went on. "One of the Indians was Wannalancet."

For a while they stood in silence. She could think of no words with which to comfort him. She tried to imagine how it must be to kill a friend. "Were you all alone?"

"No. I was with two other men. We all saw the attack start. I got there first because I can run fast."

After a pause he patted her shoulder. "What must be, must be."

"I'm so sorry, Zachary."

In the dim light she could see that he was gripping the bedpost tightly.

Finally he said, "I think I'll go down now to see Mr. Glover. You go to sleep."

"How can you go? It's so dark you won't be able to see and a lantern won't stay lit."

"I'll be all right."

He slipped out the front door so silently that Faith was certain neither Peter nor the Palmers were aware he was gone. She peered out the window after him. It was all black out. Only a man with the skills of Zachary could manage out there.

She undressed and climbed into bed, propping herself tensely against the pillows. Now that she had a husband come home she felt nervous and excited in a way she never had before, not even the night before she and Papa had set sail. What would he expect of her? What would it be like to sleep with him? Would they have a baby?

Maybe now that he was back he would wish he weren't married, especially if he heard about Peter's ideas. She bit down on her clenched fist. What would he think? If nothing else, he was bound to be angry, but perhaps he would be hurt or insulted. She twisted uneasily on the bed.

Usually she loved the sound of rain at night. Tonight its rhythm made her feel very lonely. She waited, every muscle straining, for the opening of the door.

The wind rose and sighed around the corners of the house. It whistled softly in the cracks of the windows.

The pace of rain varied: first it thudded down, battering the soil, and then with a shift in the wind it came down gently, musically. The minutes dragged on. Finally there was a gust of wind in the entry outside the parlor and the door opened.

She could barely hear his footsteps as he came into the room. Now he was hanging up his coat. She heard him at the far side of the bedstead. He must be taking a blanket out of the chest. Wasn't he going to sleep on the bedstead with her? He must have rolled up in the blanket and lain on the floor. She felt a strange combination of relief and resentment. The rain calmed again. She struggled to open her eyes just to stay awake for a few more minutes, but it was too difficult.

Faith awoke the next morning stiff and uncomfortable. The night before, when she had waited leaning up against the pillows, she had neglected to pull up the goosedown cover and had ended up sleeping with the upper half of her body uncovered. Her eyelids stuck together. She rubbed her eyes and pulled herself from the bed. There was no sign that anyone else had been in the room. The blanket, if it had been taken from the chest, had been put away again.

Most mornings Faith was the first out of bed. This morning she was the last. There was no sign of Zachary or Peter. The Palmers were sitting in front of the fire, eating hunks of cold corn porridge. They looked up with leery glances, but neither spoke. She went out to the shed to see if Blanche had been cared for.

Jester came running to greet her as soon as she opened

the door. Ears flapping, he pranced around her, rubbing his head against her legs, splashing her as he pounced into puddles. The air was fresh-washed, redolent with the fragrance of growing things. Zachary and Peter were both inside the shed. She saw Zachary talking quietly and Peter answering him with great animation.

As soon as she came closer Peter turned to her, his eyes glittering with excitement. "The sergeant is going to get a place for me in the militia, he says. I'll be able to join the group from Northfield. He says there are a lot of newcomers like me getting trained in that group."

Alarm flared in Faith's eyes as she turned to Zachary, but out of respect for Peter she said nothing.

"Faith, you milk Blanche. I'll run down to tell Rice Baldwin. The sergeant says Rice can join also."

Peter stopped milking Blanche, wiped his hands down his breeches, and rushed off downhill.

"He can't even shoot straight," said Faith, looking after him worriedly. "He's as bad as Papa was. He doesn't trip over his own feet as much as he used to, but he might endanger anyone out on a scouting party with him."

The sergeant laughed. "He's growing up fast. Peter has to go sometime. Everyone will be expecting him to, and after his experience of being kidnapped he is very eager to do his part. He'll be with Captain Turner, who is the very best officer for dealing with the younger men."

"I didn't know he wanted to go to war. He never talked about it much until last night. You are right though — he's the only man in town who has not been fighting at some time or other, except for Rice Baldwin, and he's only fifteen.''

Zachary's face was expressionless as he said, ''He probably didn't talk to you about the war because he wanted to spare you.''

Faith was startled. ''Spare me? Spare me what?''

''Spare you worrying about him, missing him if he goes.'' He looked at her searchingly. ''Will you miss him?''

''Oh, yes.'' She tried to will him to understand. ''Peter has been my only friend while you were gone. That is, except for Goody, and she is . . . well, Goody is very kind, but she has been very busy. Everyone seems to need Goody's help.''

''Goody used to spend most of her time with her family. Now that she doesn't have a family she seems to be mothering everyone else and it keeps her well occupied.''

Their conversation was interrupted by a vigorous *baaa* and a butting from Blanche. ''Oh, I had best finish the milking.'' She seated herself on the stool and firmly squeezed the teats of the goat. The milk came in steady spurts. She was proud of her milking ability and hoped that Zachary was noticing how well she did. But when she looked up at him he seemed far away.

He focused on her again. ''I'm sorry you will miss Peter,'' Zachary said in a very quiet voice.

''As long as you . . .'' she began to say, but he had gone. She heard the door close after him as he entered the house.

20 ❧ *False Impressions*

❧   "Unjust . . . that's what it is," grumbled Beatrix Palmer as she was led to the door by her husband. He looked glum but he pulled her firmly after him.

"Wait . . . wait!" insisted the angry woman. She turned and jabbed a finger in Faith's direction. "A witch, she is," she hissed. "He'd not be pushing us out 'cept for her. Look at her! That meek look is really the face of the devil."

William Palmer pulled his wife harder. "Hush, woman, you don't know what you're saying."

She opened her mouth and leaned toward Zachary, but her husband had had enough. "Silence, woman!" he bellowed. Her astonishment kept her mute until they were well away from the house.

Faith, watching from the keeping room window, kept her eyes on them until they disappeared downhill. Then she hurried to the wellsweep from which she could watch them as they set out on the road north. Only then did she give a sigh of relief.

She turned back to the house feeling as if a great weight had been lifted. The house looked more beautiful than ever. Still, there was something wrong. She drew a shaky breath. Ah, that was it — it was the woman's odor that remained.

It felt good to clean the house. Not until her hands were red and sore was the work done, but when it was, not a trace or whiff of her unwelcome guests was left.

Faith stretched her cracked red fingers. It was well worth the pain to know that her house was back to the way she wanted it. She wondered how Beatrix Palmer would take to work. She was to be a seamstress for a large family upriver and her husband was to work as a plantsman in the same home. The Reverend Mr. Glover and Goody had arranged the jobs and Mr. Glover had even been able to arrange for a militiaman who was going upriver to guide them to their new location.

A few days after they left, Peter and Rice Baldwin also left, also heading north. They had been wide-eyed and speechless with excitement. After they left Faith had cried. Peter, despite his great size, had such a thin neck and such bony wrists that he looked very young to her. It was, thought Faith, like seeing a little boy leave.

Zachary, when he saw her tears, looked stricken. She tried to explain, but he had shushed her and patted her shoulder awkwardly while she blinked the tears away. Later that evening he tried to help her with her chores and was very quiet. She understood that he was sorry for her because he thought she was in love with Peter. She did not know how to explain her feelings to him.

For two days Faith painfully missed Peter's conversation and easy company. Then she found it hard to remember him. All of her attention now centered on Zachary. She could not keep from watching him whenever he was in sight. Now that he was at home she could not see enough of him. She grew to know the way his dark hair curled flat against his neck when he sweat during his labors. She grew to know the sound of his step on the gravel of the path. As soon as she heard him coming she could picture how he would look — the flow of his body in motion, his confident stride.

Her senses were so alert to him that she could even tell his emotions by his odor. At first she could identify only the strong smell that spoke of long, arduous work, then she was also able to identify when he was angry. That scent came when he listened to people talking about the Indians in ways that enraged him.

Gradually she was able to identify a third scent — anxiety — that he most often had when he was around her. Sometimes he had it when they were working outside and shadows moved in the dark of the trees. Sometimes he had it in the evenings when faint stirrings outside brought a deadly growl from Jester lying in front of the door. More often he had it when they were sitting at meals talking and an awkwardness developed between them.

Often he assumed she was unhappy or disappointed

when she was in fact only busy or tired. She did not know how to tell him he was wrong. Shyness would grip her and if she spoke her words would be clumsy and he would misunderstand their intent.

In this uneasy way they proceeded through the sunny days during the rest of May. There were continuous reports of Indians on the warpath, and tales of tragedy came in with every visitor to the town. Toward the end of May news came of a major engagement by Turner and his men at an Indian camp north of Deerfield. Turner himself died and the English lost heavily, but the Indians suffered greater casualties.

Zachary was able to discover that neither Rice Baldwin nor Peter numbered among the casualties. He tried to convince Faith that a battle so disastrous to the Indians was probably a turning point in the war. Springfield now probably stood in less danger than it had for many months and maybe he would not need to return to action for a while.

Nonetheless, Faith was worried that Zachary would leave at any time and that they would never develop a satisfactory relationship.

She took her anxieties to Goody.

"Bless you, child, it will work out. These things have a way of resolving in the marriage bed. Just wait until you've had a bit more experience with each other and then you can show him how you feel about him."

"But, Goody, there isn't any marriage bed. I sleep in the bedstead and he sleeps in the keeping room."

Goody stopped stirring and put her hands on her ample

hips. "That bad, eh?" Her gray brows met. "Haven't the two of you ever slept together?"

Faith shook her head morosely. "I don't think he likes me," she said slowly.

Goody chuckled. "Don't be daft, girl. He can't keep his eyes off you." She shook her head. "Likely it's as you say, he thinks you love Peter and in honor doesn't feel he should take his rights. Zachary has always been a stickler for fairness.

"Humph." She fell to thinking.

"All I can suggest, Faith, is that you snuggle up to him sometime and get him kissing you. Maybe you'll be able to convince him well enough so that he'll forget his silly ideas about Peter."

Faith went back home determined to do just that.

Despite her efforts she could not get him to touch her. Daytimes she often came close to him, stumbled into him, and found reasons for reaching near or around him, but he was always able to move, as if it were some sort of a dance, just out of reach. Nighttimes there was no chance to even try for accidental touchings.

She could at least cook food he might remember her for. She spent the better part of a day laboring over a squirrel pie topped with a cornmeal crust. It was baked with the greatest care in the hot ashes of the hearth.

When the evening meal came and the pie was broken open the fragrance arose, rich and tempting. Faith watched as the steam rose before Zachary's nose. Her eyes intent on him, she leaned closer, her tongue stuck out at the corner of her mouth, and her hands clasped tightly. He raised the spoon to his mouth and then looked up and saw her intense stare. Startled, he put the spoon into his mouth too fast and burned himself.

She pulled back, aghast. "You've burned yourself!"

He choked and coughed. "I'm all right. It's very good."

"You like it?"

"Very much. It's one of the . . . it's the best pie I ever tasted—even so hot."

She sighed and sat back. He looked up again to see her still regarding him intently.

"Is there something wrong?" he asked uneasily.

She gathered her shredded courage. "You . . . you don't mind having me for a wife?"

"Mind? Why should I mind?"

She hoped her shrug looked nonchalant. "Lots of reasons. After all, you were told to marry me. And there are other women, much prettier than me, who would probably be willing to marry you."

"So?" He looked away. "I'm married to you."

She sighed deeply and looked at him from the corners of her eyes. "Since . . ." Her eyes slid away and she seemed to find her lap of great interest. "If you don't mind being married to me why . . . why don't you . . . you know . . . give me a baby?"

The silence went on so long that she boldly darted a look at him. He was looking particularly wooden. She quaked.

"You are so young."

"I'm sixteen now. I'm full grown."

"The problems of before are still with us. I might be going back to danger and leaving you alone. It would be too much for you to have a child if you were widowed at this age."

"Oh, no. Not now." She leaned forward eagerly. "Just think how awful if you were to die and your name died out. And having your baby . . . that would be a way for me to thank you for saving me."

At that he smiled. "There is no need for you to thank me. I did what I did because it was right. You should not think of having a baby as a payment. Especially since you are still so fond of Peter."

"No, no, I'm not. Well, yes, I am, but not that way." Her shoulders sagged. "If you don't give me a baby maybe no one ever will. If the war keeps on much longer there won't be any men."

He chuckled. "If there are any men left you may be certain they will notice you. You are mighty attractive, you know." She glowered at him so fiercely that he reached out and took her hand comfortingly in his. "You are very pleasing to the eye."

She hoped he could not feel her hand trembling and pulled it away so he would not notice. "I don't want just any man," she whispered.

"No, of course." His voice was prosaic. "Maybe Peter will come back even if I don't."

She turned her head away and said nothing. How much more clearly could she spell out what she wanted?

The rest of the evening passed in silence.

21 ❦ God and the Devil

❦ Faith wiggled in her seat. The sermon seemed too personal this morning. The Reverend Mr. Glover was telling the congregation that he had been inspired by a tract of the Reverend Increase Mather, whose preaching Faith had heard in Boston. Mr. Mather believed that this war with the Indians was sent to the colonists by God as a punishment for their sins. In the early days of the colony religion had been of intense interest to the colonists, but in recent years fewer people were caught up in the fear of God.

Faith had heard the same message over and over again. And it was true that she did not want to fear God, Faith thought glumly. Mr. Mather, Mr. Glover, and Papa all seemed to agree, but she could not believe that God wanted people to die in a hideous manner just to test their beliefs. She remembered the words of the kindly old vicar who had visited Auntie's long ago. He had said, "Remember these words from the scripture, child, and hold them dear all your life: 'Love one another.' ''

The people in Springfield did not seem terribly unhappy with their stern religious beliefs. Instead, they seemed pleased that God was fierce and angry. Maybe they thought that a fierce God was a strong God and therefore felt more secure with him.

Ever since the massacre there were times when she wondered if there really was a God at all. There were other times when she thought maybe God had just gone away and left them to manage as best they could in the hands of the devil.

She glanced over and caught Zachary looking at her. He gave her the faintest wink and a tiny shake of his head. She must have been sighing too loudly.

At the noontime meal Faith tried to probe Zachary's feelings about religion. "Did you agree with this morning's sermon?" she asked.

The sergeant frowned and looked uneasy. "I don't often discuss my thoughts about God. I know it is common to do so, but sometimes I disagree with the opinions of others and I believe it unseemly to cast doubt on belief that supports others."

She gnawed at her lip. "But I need to know what you think because I am so confused. Most of the people here think God wants them to suffer. I was taught that God is love."

He nodded solemnly. "It may be that evil events are more the lack of God than his intent." He frowned and thought a few minutes. "It is true that one may suffer even while experiencing God's love. That is, if he is loving he must be just, and if he is just and his law is broken, it is inevitable that punishment will follow.''

He paused, then added, ''When people feel frightened they can easily understand the wrath of God.''

She asked, ''Don't frightened people hate easily? The Palmers wanted to think all Indians are devils so they could hate them. And I haven't even seen an Indian since the massacre, but I think I would hate one if I did.''

He nodded. ''It is easy to hate. It is hard to love when there has been something like the massacre. The sights I have seen . . .'' He shook his head. ''I have also seen terrible things done to Indians by colonists. It is important to remember that such things are done by people who are hurting.''

She clenched her fists. ''You want Indians who have been faithful to the colonists to be treated decently, don't you?''

He nodded. ''Some of the Christian Indians have given up everything to help the colonists — their fellow Christians. And yet the colonists are so panicked that they are murdering them too.''

She whispered, ''Your friend Wannalancet, he was not a Christian Indian, was he?''

''No, no. He became one of King Philip's most trusted men. Because he had to choose between the colonists and his own people, he became an enemy to every Englishman — me included.''

It worried her to look at his bleak face. There was nothing she could say to make him feel better.

She felt sad for him through the rest of the day.

Toward evening Zachary asked her gently, "Do you miss Peter?"

Startled, she drew back. She did not miss Peter. A wave of shame flooded over her. How dreadful to have to admit that she was so unfeeling, so thoughtless that she had ceased thinking of Peter almost as soon as he left the house.

"Of course I miss Peter."

As soon as the words were out she realized it was a mistake to have said them. Now Zachary would think she meant she loved Peter.

Suddenly it all seemed too much. She felt guilty about Peter and about Papa. She hardly thought of Papa now. And she missed Auntie Abbie so much. And Zachary never seemed to understand her. The crying got worse and worse as if it would never stop.

Zachary's hand was on her shoulder, patting in an attempt to soothe her. She wailed louder. Why couldn't he just hug her?

Then, as her whole body wracked with sobs he did draw her into his arms and pressed her head against his shoulder. Instead of soothing her, it made her feel worse. By the time the tears subsided, she was trembling from exhaustion. She burrowed her head into his leathern jerkin and her fingers clutched the sleeves of his rough shirt.

He gently put her away from him.

"I'm sorry Peter had to leave," he said.

"Peter? Oh, Peter."

He would never understand, never. Slowly, like a

weary old woman, she set about the chores. The effort to accomplish anything became too great. She lay down on her bed, staring dry-eyed at the ceiling.

The next morning she was awakened by birdsong. Birds trilled, chirruped, and caroled all around the house. The heavy dew started drying early from the warmth of the sun. The earth smelled rich with early summer promise.

As she prepared the porridge Zachary polished his broad ax. "I'm going out to the east lot to plant corn today."

Back home in Sussex, the whole village had joined in planting. Faith remembered it with pleasure. "May I go along with you? May I help?"

He frowned down at the ax. "It's hard work, struggling with the plow."

"I helped with the planting at home."

"It was easier there."

There was a short silence. He looked up. She was still standing, watching him. Unconsciously she gave him a flirtatious glance, pulling her long plait across her cheek.

"Anyway," he went on, "you have sewing to do."

She dropped the plait and let it swing back as she stared at him in surprise. "What sewing?"

He gestured awkwardly toward her dress. "Your clothing is all too small."

She looked down. The worn fabric of her frock showed splits and gaping seams across her breasts. She darted a bashful glance at him. "I've gotten bigger since last fall. I'm taller and I've been eating more." After a pause she added, "I'm sixteen now."

He nodded. "I've spoken with Goody. She has some fabric to give you. You can busy yourself with it and it will help distract you when I'm off again."

"You're not going away again!"

"We'll see."

She felt a surge of resentment. "I'll make you a noonday meal and bring it to you."

He shook his head. "No need. I'll take a handful of corn."

When he left she glared after him. She would take him a noonday meal and it would be a good one.

She set to work on the hearth, preparing the fire, and hung the pot well above it. Slow cooking a bean stew would bring it to perfection. Zachary would not turn it down if she brought it to him. Of that she was certain.

Through the morning the birds remained so noisy that the normal sounds of the wood were quite drowned out. Jester drowsed in the sun on the doorstep and the hens scratched busily in the yard. Blanche stuck her nose over the fence and baaed her pleasure in the morning air. Trouble with Indians seemed very far away.

The morning chores done, the stew gently simmering over the banked embers, Faith called to Jester and walked over to Goody's house.

Goody was deep into the chore of cleaning out her chests. "Expected you this morning, I did," she said with her bouncing laugh. "Looked at that sunshine and said to myself, 'Zachary will surely go out planting today and will send Faith over here for that fabric.' And here it is." She leaned back with a grunt. "Oh, for the days I was as lean as you are! What with the shortage of food you would think I would be melting down more. But not me! I have to starve myself completely before I thin." She lurched upright. "Mercy!"

She caught her balance and lifted the bundle she had set atop the chest. "Here it is. This is the fabric Zachary brought back from Boston for Suzanna for the wedding they never had. Pretty, ain't it?"

Pretty! Faith turned it over in her hands. The soft, shiny silk slid delightfully against her palms. The fabric was green: a soft gray-green leaf print with intermittent leaves in a grayed blue-green.

"It's beautiful," she whispered.

"That it is," agreed Goody, all laughter gone from her voice. "My Suzanna would have looked just beautiful in it, and you will too. Zachary is fortunate to have you to wife, and all so accidental. Life is so chancy, child. My Suzanna, dead so young, and you coming out of all that horror to be a blessing to me and Zachary. You're a sweet one and no doubt of it."

A tear rolled down her cheek and she waddled over and hugged Faith. "I'll just pretend you are my daughter now, no?"

Faith hugged her back, her throat too tight for words.

Goody rubbed an arm across her eyes and stepped

back. Her accustomed laugh bubbled out. "Since you're my daughter I've got something else I've been saving for you."

She leaned over and pulled from the chest a frock of dark green and soft brown stripes. "Only a muslin it is and made down from an old one of mine, but, oh, so pretty it was on Suzanna. Just a day dress, mind you, but see, look at it against your skin. Right pretty, ain't it?"

Faith's eyes sparkled. "I know just what to do with it." She bent over and kissed the old woman's soft cheek. "Oh, thank you, Goody. I am going to hurry home now to get it ready to wear right away."

On the way home Faith hugged the dress to her and hugged, even more tightly, the feeling that Goody gave her, of being loved. Goody thought Zachary loved her, too. She said he looked at her as if he did. Maybe he was just too stuck in his shyness to tell her so.

What was it he had once said? The memory came back to her. He had said that life was a gift and we have to live it as best we can. She gave a little skip. She would tell Zachary she loved him. Then, if he loved her, he would say so.

She looked around happily. It was sunny today, the earth was alive with beauty. It brought to Faith an awareness of an order to the world: a pattern of summer and winter, autumn and spring; a pattern of growth and fullness, of decay and renewal. Thinking of these wonders she felt humbled and wondered how she could ever have questioned the existence of God. People, she thought, probably have problems because they have so many choices open to them. The world itself moved in a marvelous pattern of serenity.

For the first time since leaving England Faith felt at peace.

22 ❧ *The Rescue*

❧ The path to the field led away from the village, going directly uphill through a pine wood and down the other side of the hill along a ravine. Faith followed the drying streambed for the rest of the way. Jester, his soft ears drooping, slunk along beside her, sleepy after his lively morning. Faith carried the heavy pot of stew carefully in its towel, not wanting to stain her new dress.

The dimness of the path under the newly greening trees reminded her that this was the greatest distance she had been from the town since she had arrived in Springfield. A prickle ran across her scalp and she shuddered slightly.

As she walked Faith looked this way and that. Her whole body was tense with the strain of listening. She had not realized how much it would frighten her to be away from the town. She knew she would be terrified by any glimpse of an Indian. Goody said they used to be in and out of Springfield all the time, but Faith had not seen one since the massacre.

It did not seem very wise of Zachary to be working so far from the community. Unfortunately, almost all of the cleared fields were out from the center of things. And there weren't enough men available for them to work in groups with weapons handy.

Sunlight shone up ahead where there was a clearing. This must be the place. She held back and looked around carefully. She wanted very much to surprise Zachary. She gave Jester's nose a slight slap to warn him to go slowly and went forward noiselessly on her moccasined feet to the laurel at the edge of the wood. Someone was working rhythmically in the sunlight of the clearing. She could hear the grunt as an ax cut deeply, and she moved until she saw Zachary bent over, straining at the handle of his ax, now caught in a root.

At the same moment he entered her line of vision, so too did a smooth-shaven head but ten feet in front of her, slowly rising out of the depth of the laurel. Zachary was pulling back on the ax, the muscles of his bare arms glistening in the sun. She could see only one Indian and Jester was pointing in that direction, so she guessed he was the only one about. The Indian was moving cautiously, probably because he was afraid Zachary would gain control of the ax.

Now he was moving stealthily forward, his tomahawk raised.

In the months since the massacre Faith had relived over and over that time of horror and wondered how she would feel, what she would think, if such a thing threatened again. Now facing the loss of Zachary she was not aware of thinking or feeling. All her energy was concentrated on what she could do.

With a great scream of warning she threw herself forward. As she leapt, she flung the hot iron pot full of steaming stew straight at the Indian's head.

She had leapt too quickly and too far to be able to keep her balance. She fell sprawling on the forest floor, her face skidding into the moist leaves. She heard a harsh gasp, a grunt, thrashing in the laurel, and then feet thudding across the clearing. Her heart started thumping, hurting in her chest.

Jester's high-pitched bay came from the other side of the clearing. Gradually it faded off into the forest beyond.

Faith pulled herself up, wiped the dirt from her face, and looked around. She was certain she had hit the Indian, but he had disappeared and so had Zachary. The sunlight shimmered in the clearing. From where she stood, only the disturbed leaves at her feet gave any indication that anything had happened.

She stepped forward cautiously. The iron pot had rolled into a hole. She looked more carefully. Beans were scattered all around.

Her knees were limp and her head felt light. She reached for the reassuring hardness of a tree trunk and clung to it. The bad feeling passed but she was shaking all over. She pressed her forehead into the sharp bark and made herself breathe slowly.

A bird chirped and she realized why she had felt so uneasy walking along — the birds, after their racket this morning, had stilled.

Surely it had been only one Indian. When would Zachary return? She scanned the area with care. The leaves on the trees were still too thin to conceal a person. Only the laurel could have hidden anyone and she could see that no one was there.

Faith leaned against the tree and waited. Gradually the woodland began to come alive. Birds seldom sang in the full of the afternoon, as they had earlier, but now they began making soft chirrups and twitters, fussing among the leaves. Small creatures stirred and she felt, rather than heard, the murmur of the forest.

It was some minutes before Zachary reappeared. He came striding through the woods, dappled sunlight brightening his jerkin to pale brown. Sudden tears of relief came to her eyes and she ran across the clearing, jumping from hummock to hummock. Breathless, she flung herself at him. His arms steadied her and tightened around her as she put her head down, hearing the beating of his heart. He had been running fast.

"He's gone. Got clear away." He caught his breath. "Followed him as far as the river where he decided to swim. I saw his head far out — but not so far that I could not see the large lump forming on it. We won't see him again."

"Are you sure?"

"It's not likely. That was Sassamin, brother to Wannalancet. He too used to be a friend but he wanted, of course, to avenge his brother's death. But it is more and more dangerous for Indians around here. As much as he might want to, he'll not risk returning, knowing I'm on the lookout for him.'' Zachary seemed as wound up and shaky as she was. ''Anyway, he's badly injured. What did you hit him with?''

''The small bean pot,'' she said proudly as they went back across the clearing hand in hand.

''You see?'' She picked it up and displayed it. One lone bean clung to the lip. It was still hot.

''How . . . ?''

''I had just come. He moved so fast I didn't have the time to warn you or grab a stone or anything else.''

His hand tightened. ''You saved my life. I had allowed myself to be far away in thought.'' He looked around at the spilled beans. ''I'm glad the hot beans didn't fly back at you.''

He lifted her chin and studied her face with concern.

She swallowed hard. ''I wouldn't care,'' she said vehemently. ''I would do anything for you!''

''You . . . ?''

''Of course. You're the most important person in the world to me.''

''I am? What about Peter?''

''Peter? Peter! Do you think that I feel this way about Peter? He's like a brother!''

His hands tightened on her arms. His voice was rough. ''You care that much for me?''

She nodded wordlessly.

He whitened under his tan. ''It's hard to believe.''

She hiccupped. "Don't you understand that I feel safer and happier with you than I do with anyone else, and I trust you? I want to belong to you and I want you to belong to me. I love you."

He ran the tips of his fingers over her face as if he were blind and getting to know her. "Are you sure?"

"I'm sure. I'm so glad I am married to you." Here her voice grew stronger and she even surprised herself as she said, "Because of you I am even glad that I left my Auntie Abbie and came to the colony."

He started to smile and the smile got bigger and bigger. The tanned skin around his eyes crinkled up and, close as she was, she saw green and blue and yellow in the irises of his eyes. He was looking at her as if he could never get enough of seeing her.

Her voice cracked as she asked, "Do you . . . do you care for me much?"

His eyes never left hers. "I love you," he said.

She gave a laugh of sheer joy. Her heart started thumping hard again. "You mean it? You love me enough to want to be married to me?"

He took a quick breath. "You are the best thing that ever happened to me."

She gripped tightly on his jerkin. "Can I be a real wife? Can we try to have a baby?"

"Now . . . I . . . you . . . yes."

She leaned forward and kissed him quickly. The kiss landed on the side of his nose.

He drew her close. The next kiss lasted so long that

only the sound of Jester, crashing through the under-
brush, broke them apart.

He looked all around and then smiled. "That dog
makes as much noise as a bear."

She came back to his arms. He kept kissing her until
they were hot in the sun. "I'm hot," she said and tugged
him over to the shade at the edge of the woodland.

"You're beautiful," he said, wiping back the tendrils
that stuck to her forehead. "And that dress — such a
pretty dress. I've never seen it before."

She looked down at it ruefully. "Goody gave it to
me this morning. It was so pretty, but look, when I fell
it ripped." She looked up and was startled by the intense
look in his eyes. Suddenly shy, she picked up the bean
pot. "Maybe we should go home. You haven't eaten
and the stew is all spilled."

"Yes, I'll come." He picked up his ax. "It's time
to make definite plans for staying. I'll talk with the
militia this afternoon. They wanted me to be an officer
of the garrison here, but I thought it might be better if
I went back out again as a guide. I didn't think I could
stand living here with you if you were yearning after
Peter. Now I'll tell them I have decided to stay."

"You're not going to leave me. Oh, Zachary!" She
gave a little jump for the joy of it.

His laugh sounded almost lighthearted.

"I didn't want to leave you, but going would, of
course, be one way of keeping you safe." His hand
tightened on her arm. "I will do whatever is necessary

so that horrors like High Hills won't happen anymore.'' He stopped, dropped the ax, and pulled her tightly into his arms. ''I don't know how I could stand it if anything happened to you.''

''Things aren't ever going to be so bad again, are they Zachary?''

''Praise God, they never will. They say all wars are terrible, but to me this seems as bad as they can get. Brother against brother it is, because the Indians have, many of them, been our brothers. Oh Faith, I hate fighting them, but we have no choice.''

They turned and headed toward home.

''Hard as things are,'' said Faith, ''we need only to deal with them one day at a time. The Bible says, 'Sufficient unto the day is the evil thereof.' ''

He grunted. ''It is a wise quotation. There is also another one I remember, 'Weeping may endure for a night, but joy cometh in the morning.' Our joy is coming.''

His hand tightened on hers as they walked. Faith noticed that they kept the same pace.